TRIGGER

By
Scarlett Dawn

This is a work of fiction. Names, characters, places and incidents are either the product of the author's imagination or used fictitiously, and any resemblance to actual persons, living or dead, business establishments, events or locales is entirely coincidental.

To my fans.

Scarlett Dawn

New York Times bestselling author, Scarlett Dawn, has created a fresh and magical new adventure for romance and paranormal lovers alike. Shifters now run the world through corporations after the humans all but destroyed Earth. It's too bad humans are still oblivious. They have no clue terrifying beasts rule their broken world.

And then along came a human. A beautiful and klutzy human.

She's the trigger the shifters have been waiting for...

But beware of the soul-sucking darkness soon to follow.

CONTENTS

CHAPTER ONE

"Are you going to beg again?" Logan asked. His cheeks pinched as he grinned. This man who was checking my electronic bracelet to allow me entry to the compound knew full well my dilemma. He had to listen to me complain every time I marched outside for air, after an argument with my father. "You have less than two days before you're screwed."

My face scrunched up in irritation. "I have a different plan if my father says no this time."

His silver hair gleamed in the fading light of the setting sun. "That would be?"

I shook my head ever so slowly. "It would probably be best if you didn't know."

"You're not going to kill him, are you?" One bushy eyebrow rose.

"No." My brown eyes rolled. "I do love the bastard."

"Just don't do anything illegal," he rumbled. He patted my back as his scanner beeped in confirmation that I had access—of course, I did. I had lived on bases like this my entire life. His beefy right hand opened the door for me after he tapped in the code. "I worry about you, Poppy."

I walked inside, mumbling, "Don't. I'm a big girl now. I can handle myself."

"Be careful! I mean it," he hollered after me.

The door *shushed*, closing out the fallen world.

I shook my head and tightened my ball cap on my head as I went through the body scanner. The guards there waved as I went through, gifting me encouraging smiles. Even I knew it was sad how the military personnel here were more fatherly than my own parent was. But I would take matters into my own hands if it came down to it. Because Logan was right. Time was running out.

I had turned into a selfish bitch the last few years.

It didn't bother me any. If I wanted my freedom, I had to be ruthless.

My father no longer had access to my hard-earned money. Not that I had much, but I had saved to do what I must if he said no tonight. I would *not* be stuck here forever.

* * *

My rump was almost numb by the time my father walked into our quarters. I had been sitting in wait at the dining room table for just this moment. His red uniform, decorated with medals, shone in the bright kitchen overhead lighting. My father may be a pain most of the time, but he knew how to intimidate in his finery. All of his subordinates were scared of him.

I used to be too.

Now I was just pissed.

"Hello, Father," I stated with false cheer. "How was your day?"

He opened the fridge and ducked to peer inside it, the inside light showing the wrinkles on his forehead. "I know that tone, darling dearest." His brown eyes flicked in my direction as he pulled a bottle of water from the depths of the cooling unit. He kicked the door closed with ease and turned to face me. His throat worked as he took a long drink from the bottle, staring over the edge at me.

He grinned full of mirth. "What is it that you want this time?"

I tilted my head and cracked my neck. "Who says I want anything?"

"Pretty much every time you're waiting for me after work, you want something."

My red brows furrowed. "Really?"

"Really." His black shoes clicked on the tiling as he walked toward me. His strong hand pulled out the chair next to me, taking a seat. Eyes identical to my own stared into my soul. "I can guess what it's about this time."

I stayed silent.

He rubbed at the wrinkles in his forehead absently as he leaned back, getting comfortable. "We've had this discussion a hundred times. I won't sign off on you entering the Corporate Army."

I kept my expression serene, not showing any of the frustration racing inside my head. "But you would sign off on me marrying a stranger? A stranger who is in your army?"

His voice was as calm as my façade. "He isn't a stranger. I know him well. He's a good man for you to marry. And it's a good thing he works for the Liberated Army. You know that." He swallowed another large drink of his water, and then he sighed. "Does it help that he's a good-looking man?"

"I don't care what he looks like." Though I was surprised my father had taken the time to make sure the man he chose for me was 'good looking.' I hadn't expected that. "And I don't care what the laws are. I don't want to marry a stranger. The only way for me to stay single is to join the Corporate Army. You know that."

This time, he stayed silent.

I jumped on his hesitancy. "Father, you've trained me well. You know I'll make the cut. I'll pass, and I'll have my freedom."

He instantly shook his head. "Working for the Corporations is not freedom."

My temperature started to rise, staining my cheeks pink. "And neither is an arranged marriage."

"I know that, Poppy!" He jerked to stand and grabbed his water with a hard hand. "But I would rather have you marry someone I know is a good man than to have you be a slave to the Corporations. Don't you understand that? They killed your mother. Or have you forgotten that little detail?"

"No. I haven't forgotten." I ducked my face and leaned my elbows on the table. I stared at my clasped hands. Ever so slowly, I shook my head, my voice quiet. "I don't want to marry a stranger. I can't. I won't. And I only have a day and a half left before I'm too old to join the Corporate Army."

"And there's only a few weeks left before you must say 'I do.' By law. I've waited as long as I could. But you're almost twenty-five now. You didn't pick anyone to marry, so I made the hard choice for you."

No, I was making the hard choice.

I continued to gaze at my clasped hands. "I wish you would reconsider."

"I can't. I *won't*, as you said." He turned and walked back into the kitchen. "I have a meeting I'm getting ready for, so don't disturb me. I'll be working until later tonight."

"Father?" I glanced up, pleading with my eyes. "Please..."

He shook his head one last time. "No." His eyes scanned my face, softening a minor degree. "Your fiancé will be here tomorrow. You'll be able to meet him then. I promise you that I've picked the best I can. I do believe you'll like him."

My eyes widened to the extreme. "Tomorrow?"

He nodded. "Yes, I thought it would be best for you two to have a few days together before..." He trailed off and sighed. "Well, you'll get to meet him soon enough."

I could only gawk at my father.

"He truly is handsome." He winked as he exited into his office.

Fuck. Me.

CHAPTER TWO

I punched a code into the door, my fingers shaking with anger. The light turned green. I jerked the long handle sideways and exhaled in appreciation as the large food locker's freezing air hit my face. I stepped from the loading dock into the refrigeration unit and took my time winding through the maze of product. When my skin was properly chilled and no longer flushed with frustration, I walked through the far door and into a dimly lit hallway.

The walls were painted ivory, and the floor was made of dark silver concrete. It was a hallway I'd stumbled through—in a drunken stupor—many times. I walked with forced patience, more than ready to sit down where there were plenty of bottles of alcohol. The burn of hard liquor running down my throat would be a welcome sweet agony.

A right turn took me to the back entrance of my favorite bar on base. Typically, it was filled with military personnel I knew well. But tonight, I stopped just past the door and glanced around. The walls of this place were paper thin, so I tried not to listen as a man peed inside the bathroom on my left. There were many individuals—every single one a male—sitting at the bar and at the free standing tables, all chatting amicably.

But they weren't wearing the red uniforms of the Liberated Army.

The soldiers wore black military attire, a golden crown stitched on the material.

It was the Corporate Army.

I pulled my ball cap down a little further on my head as a few peered in my direction.

I had apparently walked in on their private party.

It wasn't the first time I had done such. There were always different groups coming onto the base to meet with officials here. I just hadn't expected it tonight.

My favorite bartender waved in my direction. "What'll it be tonight, Poppy?"

Guilt for crashing their party made me hesitate.

Gina coaxed, "Come on, girl. I know you need a drink. I can see it on your face."

I strolled toward her and sat on one of the two vacant high seats at the end of the curved bar. Gina was right. I did need a drink. Or three. Maybe a bottle or ten. Who knew how trashed I would be by the time I left here.

The bathroom door opened and shut behind me, and the place quieted down noticeably.

I leaned on the bar and dropped my forehead onto a crooked arm. I groaned. "I'll take two shots of whiskey and a beer. To start with."

She whistled loud. "It must have been a hell of a night so far."

I peeked up at her from my arm. "My dad is dead set. He won't change his mind."

The man who had exited the bathroom brushed my arm as he sat down on the remaining empty seat in the bar. I slow-blinked as the occupants of the place chattered on with gusto once more. I rubbed at my left ear with annoyance. They were damn loud.

"Did you put up a calm argument?" Gina questioned. She placed my two shots down in front of my face and lifted a beer from the cooler under the bar. It, too, was sat in front of me. "I told you that you needed to speak rationally to him."

"I took your advice." I bounced my forehead against my forearm twice and growled. "My father is an absolute overbearing, stubborn ass. I thought I almost had him, and then he put up the brick wall."

There was a quiet grunt from the man next to me, the one who had brushed my arm. "Most fathers are a pain. I have one myself who I would categorize just as you did yours." He paused, and stated, "Gina, I'll take another beer, please."

My attention perked as the man spoke. His accent was delicious. I'd never heard it before, and I had been many places in my twenty-four—almost twenty-five—years on this wretched war-torn earth. The tones of his voice were like honey and chocolate, each syllable fighting for the most delectable cadence.

My favorite bartender was breathless as she answered, "Coming right up."

He must be a looker for her to act that way. She was the most married of married here on base. Thirty years of marriage, four children, and ten grandchildren. Gina was exactly what the marriage law had in mind when it was enacted almost one hundred years ago. A woman to help populate the earth again after we all but destroyed ninety percent of the population from war. A broodmare, for lack of a better term. But Gina actually loved her husband, and he loved her. They were a perfect match, even all these years later.

I sat up on my chair fully and lifted one of my shot glasses to the right. *To the man who had sat down next to me.* All I could see from under the bill of my ball cap was a deep gray suit. It appeared to be made of the finest material too. He was definitely corporate in that outfit, and a higher-up corporate, but I didn't see many men who wore it quite so well. It fit him snug in his broad shoulders, and where he had unbuttoned the jacket, his white dress shirt was snug against a flat, trim stomach. His gray slacks hugged his thighs to perfection. The suit was indeed tailored to fit him; it was an extension of his powerful physique.

This man was rich in a world that lived in poverty.

He was everything my father hated.

"To overbearing fathers?" I asked, lifting my shot glass a little higher.

The man chuckled, and it was like a sultry night on satin sheets. He raised the beer Gina had left for him before she blushed and scurried to the other end of the bar. A dark tan hand, strong with perfectly manicured fingernails, angled his beer against my shot glass. The two clinked together under the low-hanging light.

He returned, "To overbearing fathers."

We both tipped our drinks back in agreement of our toast. The whiskey warmed my throat just as I'd needed tonight. I pushed the empty glass away from me and pulled my beer closer.

I twirled my drink in slow motion and stared down the neck of the bottle to the golden alcohol, my anger rising once more. If my father just had listened, I wouldn't have needed to plan my escape tonight. I wouldn't have needed to forge his name on the Corporation Army's enlistment—which was illegal in all the wrong ways. Now, I would be leaving him behind for a future he did not want for me.

"Speak again," the man stated.

My brows puckered, but I didn't look up from my stare down with my drink. "Why?"

He didn't immediately answer. But when he did, it was quiet. "Your voice doesn't hurt my ears."

I chuckled. "That's a new one."

His shoulders shrugged. "It's the truth." He took another drink from his beer. "What's your name?"

"Poppy."

"That's new." He grunted and took another drink. "Last name?"

I didn't hesitate to give him my middle name. I didn't like people knowing I was the daughter of the great General Carvene. "My name's Poppy Bree."

He reciprocated in kind. "I'm Godric Leon."

I took a slow swig of my beer, closing my eyes just to listen to that delicious voice of his. "Are you here on business, Godric?"

"I am. You?"

I peered down at my simple navy cargo pants and white t-shirt. I laughed outright imagining myself going to a meeting with the legendary General Carvene dressed as I was.

"No. I live here on base."

When he took the longest drink so far, I waited. Just waited, with my eyes now open, for him to speak in that beautiful accent. He sat his beer down very gradually and paused. He leaned closer to me, and I didn't move as he stole my remaining shot of whiskey.

When he downed that, he asked evenly, "Are you married, Poppy?"

The bar quieted once more, and I glanced in the direction of the throng. They were still talking, but it seemed more passive. Or perhaps I was just getting used to their disorderly group. I shook my head and pushed my beer away. I knew where this was going.

"No, I'm not married. Not yet, anyway." I flicked a finger at him. "You?"

"I've never been married." He drummed his fingers on the bar, his long tan fingers. "Your age?"

"Old enough."

"For?"

"What you're about to ask me next."

More drumming of his fingers. "I need your age, Poppy." He didn't pretend ignorance.

I liked that about him.

"I'm twenty-four."

His fingers stopped drumming. "And you're not married?"

"Not yet," I repeated.

His pointer finger started drawing invisible circles on the wooden bar. "Is that why your father is an overbearing asshole?"

I pulled my beer back to me. "I guess this isn't going where I thought it was."

His laughter tickled my ears in the most pleasant way, deep with a rumble of an entertained man. "All right. No more talking about your father." His pointed finger made those lazy circles on the scarred wood. His voice lowered to a dominant purr. "Would you like to leave here with me?"

I took one last drink of my beer. "To have sex?"

I could be blunt too.

"Yes." There was seductive humor in his tone.

The noise had definitely died down in the bar.

I peered out into the crowd, but no one was looking this way. I pushed my beer away from me once more. "You haven't even seen my face."

"And you haven't looked at mine either."

True. "Then why?"

He shrugged. "I like your voice."

My lips curved up. "I like yours too."

"So?" Godric waited with patience I didn't have.

"Yes, I'll leave with you for a few hours."

My father would hate this choice. A corporate man.

A corporate *rich* man.

That made him perfect to have a romp with before I left this place. My anger would have a nice outlet...and release. Plus, I might as well see if these corporate men were any good in bed—since I was headed to New City, anyway. That was all they had there. It was time to give them a good ol' test drive.

CHAPTER THREE

Godric turned, slid from his chair, and buttoned his suit jacket in one fluid move. "Let's go."

A little bossy, but I didn't mind.

I was on a time crunch.

"Gina, put my drinks on my tab," I hollered.

She nodded and waggled her eyebrows, fully knowing what I was doing.

I turned and slid off my seat, not nearly as gracefully as he had.

When I landed, my right foot slammed on top of his left one. He didn't complain. He merely pulled his shiny shoe out from underneath my sneaker and grabbed ahold of my shoulders, steadying me. His hands fell to his sides as I stared at his massive chest. I was almost eye level with it. He was much larger than I had thought.

He grunted. "Are you sure you're twenty-four?"

"Yes." I straightened my shoulders. I knew I wasn't tall.

"Were you hit with the short stick as a child?" Humor laced his tone.

I snorted. "Did you eat magic beans as a child? You're like an ogre."

His chest vibrated in front of my gaze, the white shirt stretched lovingly over his muscles. His laughter was a pure delight. He raised his right hand and tapped one finger on the edge of my hat. "Take it off.

I'd like to see you now." It was a soft order.

My fingers twitched as I peered back to the other occupants of the bar. They weren't looking this way, and we were in the back. But my father had always told me to keep my hair up around men. He said I was too pretty for my own good. Whatever that meant.

"Are you hideous under there?" he teased playfully, sensing my hesitation.

I ground my teeth together and yanked my ball cap off. My long red waves fell over my shoulders to the middle of my back in a rush of freedom. I shook my head a little, so they weren't as crushed, and then I peered up into the face of the bossy corporate man.

The crushed skyscrapers outside the base must have swayed, a strong wind rattling their infested dwellings, because the world danced a beautiful melody under my feet and my knees weakened. The axis that I judged all men upon tilted and crashed. I couldn't move. I could barely breathe.

He. Was. Magnificent.

His skin was the color of cocoa mixed with rare marshmallows, perfectly tan from a distinctive heritage. His eyes tilted just at the ends, like an Egyptian god. His nose was strong like his jawline was proud. The lips that created such beautiful tones from regular words were lush and red. And his hair... it was tawny with golden highlights, the loose curls down to his giant shoulders. He appeared near my age, a little older. Probably thirty.

But his eyes held my attention.

I stared. And he stared right back, not looking away.

Gold eyes with flecks of amber held my brown gaze.

His penetrating gaze was extraordinary against his complexion. This man was flawless.

Time passed—flew, really.

Maybe a second. Maybe a minute. Maybe ten.

Neither of us spoke.

My mouth finally bobbed. I croaked, "Yeah, you'll do."

His blink was so slow it was near lethargic. "Yes. I suppose you'll do, too." Those golden eyes with amber splashes ran down my slim frame, his perfect eyebrows pinching together. "I may be too much for you, though." His words were quiet, not bragging—just truthful.

"There's only one way to find out." I gestured toward the front door. "After you."

Any hesitancy evaporated from his gaze, his attention sharpening on my eyes. "Actually, I'd love to see how you snuck in here. Those front doors are locked."

I shrugged and turned back the way I had come in. "Follow me then." I waved my hat in the air and peered over my shoulder. "But we're not going to my quarters right now. Not unless you'd like to meet my overbearing father. He's working in there right now."

His words were dry. "As much fun as that sounds, I'd rather not."

I snickered and opened the back door. "I didn't think you would. He would be a mood killer." Understatement.

My father would probably pull one of his deadly swords and ruin the handsome corporate man's face. That would be the real tragedy. This ugly world needed beauty like his. And my father would laugh with glee, wiping it away, if he saw this man headed to my bedroom.

Shadows danced at our feet as we walked down the ivory hallway. I glanced back quickly, palming the handle of the knife strapped to my right thigh. But I paused in pulling it, eyeing the two Corporate Army soldiers who trailed us. "They're yours?"

"Yes." He didn't even look back. "The others will be along shortly."

Others? How many guards did this man warrant?

He eyed the next door I stopped in front of and

evaluated the room through the window. "We're going in here?"

"Yeah. It's our exit." I opened the door to the food locker, the blast of cold air ruffling my hair. "This way."

He plucked an apple from a bin and munched as he followed. "Are there any more exits to the bar?"

"One other one. But it smells. No one goes that way unless you're unloading trash."

"The trash shoot."

"Yes."

"Too small to enter from."

I grinned and punched in the code at the back door. "Not for me."

He leaned forward and pressed his chest to my back, and grabbed the door handle. His heat burned against my chilled shoulder. "Allow me."

The door swung open with ease as he pushed.

I usually had to put a little muscle into it.

"Thank you," I whispered. I stepped into the warmth outside the cooling unit.

"Where to now?" he asked, peering around the loading dock.

I pointed to the door ten feet away. "That'll take us to the lobby."

He raked his gaze back to his men and tossed them the apple core, finished with his snack. He barely tipped his head to the door and flicked one finger. They were shutting the door to the walk-in refrigerator and leaving us alone on the dock in a blink, disappearing back to the bar.

My brows rose. "No guards?"

Godric snorted. "There are always guards outside of New City."

When we stepped through the door into the lobby, I choked on air.

He repeated himself, "Always guards."

I hurried to put my ball cap back on. All thirty-plus of the Corporate Army soldiers who had been in the bar were now waiting in the lobby. Their eyes were averted from us while they surveyed the Liberated Army roaming the main floor.

I sputtered, "They're all for you?"

"Yes," Godric muttered, not too pleased with it. He placed a proprietary palm at the small of my back, guiding us to the center of the guards. They were all buff like the man I was with, but Godric still seemed so much more. It made me take pause and wonder if I really would be able to make the cut in this army.

I leaned toward him as they all started moving—us with them. I whispered, "What the hell do you do within the corporations to get stuck with this much detail?"

Golden eyes peered down at me. "Remember my overbearing ass of a father?"

I nodded.

He flicked a hand at the guards, full of arrogance. "This is his doing."

"Ah." I nodded again as if he hadn't evaded the question rather beautifully.

Not only was he the best-looking man I had ever seen, but he was also intelligent.

The way the guards took the stairs was a movement of magnificence, all walking as one in front of us and behind. I stumbled on a step, not paying attention, and Godric pulled me closer to his side.

He sniffed in my direction, and then questioned, "Are you drunk? Did you drink before you entered the bar?"

I held my head higher. "No."

He snorted, and looked away, but kept his arm close around me. "Then you're a klutz."

I ground my teeth together. "Only sometimes."

"It's been twice so far in the past ten minutes."

"Sometimes...might be a loose term."

Godric snickered. "Honesty with one's self is most important."

The guards turned in the opposite direction of my

quarters, and I breathed a sigh of relief. If we had gotten any closer, my father's guards would have taken notice of the entourage—with me in the middle of it. They would have taken offense to be sure. I was sure no one wanted a sword fight happening in the cramped hallway of the housing area.

We eventually stopped turning down multiple passages and headed straight to a door at the end of the hall. The section we were now in was reserved for the VIP business associates. The typically bland colors decorating the halls turned decadent and vibrant, the carpeting now plush under my sneakers. This area was meant to seduce the eye and coax visitors into relaxation. My father had always said that where a man lays his head for the night could mean either pampered friends or stubborn enemies in the boardroom. Hence, why he kept this area pretty-pretty for the corporate snobs that battled with him across a conference table.

The guards parted and placed their backs to the wall, clearing an area for Godric and me to walk forward. Two of his guards were already searching his room, not yet giving the all clear to enter.

My lips trembled in amusement. I stood up on tiptoe to whisper, "They're just going to stay out here while we do the funky monkey?" Those doors weren't soundproof.

He peered at each guard before us, some with suspiciously shaking shoulders as if they had heard my whispered comment. He flat out glared with death's own blade at all of them and ground his teeth together. He finally muttered, "Yes. They won't leave. These unloyal bastards work for my father, not me." He cleared his throat. "But I do pay them enough on the side that they'll keep their mouths shut. This will be between you and me. No one else."

"Well, I'll just need to be extra quiet," I mumbled under my breath.

The guards exited his room and nodded their

heads.

Godric led me into his room, shutting the door behind us. He walked straight to the oversized bed in the center of the room, unbuttoning his suit jacket as he went. It dropped on the floor. He turned and leaned a hip against the side of the mattress and started to undo the buttons on his white shirt.

His head tilted to the bed, his blazing eyes on mine. "Are you coming?"

When his shirt hit the floor, and he revealed the torso of a man who knew how to take care of himself— *muscles all along that tan flesh*—I started unstrapping myself of weapons and nodded.

"Fuck yes."

CHAPTER FOUR

Godric picked me up next to the bed and slammed my back against the wall. I grunted in pain, but he didn't apologize. His mouth instantly landed on my tender neck, and he placed a hard kiss on my flesh, his warm, plump lips crushing against my skin. The tip of his nose trailed up to my ear while he inhaled deeply. He hissed, "You smell good enough to devour, pet."

"Oh, God," I moaned, pressing my body flush against his. He didn't smell so bad himself. Wildness and spice, with a hint of cherries. I groaned and tilted my head to the side as his teeth bit my earlobe.

The click of metal had my eyes lowering, to the object he had taken from the back of his pants, as he placed it on the bedside table. I hadn't noticed any blades on him before, and this item I was unfamiliar with.

I asked, "What's that?"

"A weapon." He pulled my t-shirt off over my head. Golden eyes flared on the soft mounds of flesh at the top of my bra. He ran one heated finger against my heaving breasts. A shiver ran down my spine at his hard demand, powerful and sinful. "Don't touch it."

I arched against the wall while goose bumps pebbled on my skin. His lone finger rubbed gentle circles on my small cleavage, and I whimpered for more.

My words were breathless. "What kind of

weapon?"

"The dangerous kind." His olive skin rippled with lickable muscles as he lifted me again and tossed me on the bed—away from the unknown weapon. Golden eyes full of heat burned into my exposed skin while I scooted to the center of the bed. He yanked off one of my sneakers and then the other. Godric licked his bottom lip, his gaze lingering between my thighs. "Are you protected from pregnancy, pet?"

I nodded and lifted my silver bracelet in front of my face. With a simple punch of a code, it scanned my body while he pulled my socks from my feet.

I tilted my arm in his direction so he could view the readout. "No diseases. And I'm set for six more months on birth control."

He stopped unzipping my pants to type in a code on his own silver bracelet. The readout he showed indicated he was free of all diseases too. "No condoms then?"

"No condoms," I agreed.

Skin on skin was a wicked indulgence.

Godric leaned down and placed his strong arms on either side of my body. He bit the waistline of my pants and peered up with the navy material still between his teeth.

My breath caught. This man wanted to consume me. So much desire radiated off him, in waves of heat, that I lifted my hips just to be closer to his warmth.

He tugged the material with his white teeth before releasing it and licking along my waistline just above my pants, his pink tongue appearing between his red lips.

"In the bar, you said you only had a few hours. How many?" Godric questioned.

"Maybe two." I wiggled beneath him. I unhooked my bra and let it fall off the side of the bed. "Maybe less."

"Let's make the best of it then," Godric purred.

There was a slight draft coming from the air

conditioner overhead, but the cool air would feel wonderful in just a few minutes. His muscles clenched as he pulled my pants down, my panties going with them. They were tossed aside, and I was naked before him.

Godric rose to his knees on the bed and gradually unbuckled his black belt. Hungry golden eyes stared down at my skin, eating up every secret spot on my body. His lips curved up at the edges, a hint of sensual delight. He was enjoying the view as he unbuttoned and unzipped his dress slacks.

I grinned in appreciation and sat up, pressing my palms to his chest. His warm pecs were dark compared to my porcelain skin. The pads of my fingers dipped over his hardened muscles; they were glorious and lethal, pure power all in one man. I peered up into his eyes as I played with one of his tiny brown nipples.

I whispered with honesty, "You are gorgeous."

He pressed his lips lightly on my forehead, before removing the rest of his clothing. "The same could be said for you."

I wasn't prepared when he placed his right hand on the center of my chest and shoved me back flat on the bed. A shocked grunt escaped, and I stared at him wide-eyed. But he was already dipping his head to my breasts. He may have been right. He may be too much for me.

Except the man had a fantastic tongue. Godric's mouth captured my left breast and sucked without remorse while one of his hands cupped my right one. His mouth and tongue tortured me on one side, and on the other, he was gentle and careful as he molded my flesh. His resulting groan had my eyes rolling up in my head, the cadence of his voice just as stimulating.

My hands lifted and my fingers threaded through his tawny hair. It was soft but not as soft as mine. Each fine strand had a coarseness to it that matched this man's wicked ways. I hissed as his teeth latched onto my nipple with enough bite to make my muscles clench. Then he ran his pink tongue over the sting and sucked my nipple softly into his mouth.

I spread my legs and wrapped them around his body as his mouth traveled south down my stomach. His tongue circled my belly button three times before he nipped at the soft skin there. I giggled from the touch, a ticklish spot, and he fluttered his fingers over it while his face dipped between my thighs. I was stuck between wiggling and laughing or tossing my head back in a pleasured shout.

It came out as a choked groan, loud and long.

He snickered gently.

I smacked his forehead softly. "Mean."

"More than you know," he whispered.

Then his sinful mouth was on my core, and I couldn't speak any longer. No complaints passed my lips. Every lap of his tongue, each moan rumbled from his chest, every flick of his finger against my clit elicited a shouting, shivering mess.

So much for being quiet.

His large, strong hands gripped my thighs and held them apart with ease when my legs clamped down on the sides of his head. My fingers clenched his hair, but he didn't care. He only groaned more fiercely when I yanked his face closer, tightening my grip even further on his tawny curls.

"Quit teasing, Godric," I panted.

His lips curved against my intimate flesh.

My body bowed hard off the bed, his mouth sucking fiercely on my clit and two of his fingers spearing up into my vaginal opening. The world ceased to exist, all noise disappeared as fire shot through my system, igniting pleasure in every cell of my body. My entire being shook as wave after wave of bliss pulled me under into the most enjoyable sated warmth.

My eyes opened wide when he abruptly lifted my

body, as if I weighed nothing, and bashed my back against his headboard. I opened my mouth on a keening cry as he drove his cock—his thick and long as hell cock—up into my tight core. One thrust. Two. Three, and he was totally seated inside me.

He tensed to move, holding me close.

I smacked at his shoulder. And with a rapid breath, I sputtered, "Just a second. Wait, wait!"

Golden eyes full of lust pinned me in place—not like his huge cock wasn't already. All of his beautiful muscles froze, barely constraining his need to keep going.

His nostrils flared, and he hissed as he said, "Are you shitting me, pet?"

I blinked my gaze of desire and shook my head quickly. I whispered as quietly as I could, "I'm not stopping-stopping you." I jerked my head toward his door behind him, sensual sweat causing our bodies to slide against each other. A small amount of light from the hallway was peeking inside his room from the ajar door. "Your door is cracked open."

CHAPTER FIVE

His striking eyes narrowed.

I froze like a mouse hunted by a cat.

Whoever had opened his door…

Well, I was glad I wasn't that person.

He turned his head to the side, and barked, "What the fuck do you want, Jonathan?"

A throat cleared from outside. "Sir, we've been informed your meeting is finally scheduled; it's in five minutes."

Godric kept his attention turned to the side, glaring at the wall—no longer at me. He ground his teeth together even as his gripping arms around my legs pulled me closer, his cock pushing deeper into my channel. "Tell that goddamn asshole he can wait. And shut my door. Now."

I bit my bottom lip to keep from moaning in pleasure. His cock was just the right size that the sensation was between pleasure and pain. Perfectly proportioned for my body.

Jonathan argued, "Sir, he stated—"

"I don't give two fucks what he said." Godric shouted, "Shut my damn door. Or I will bury your furry, motherfucking, unloyal, shit-for-brains ass so far in the ocean, no one will ever find you!"

The door clicked shut—quickly.

I blinked a few times at his profile and attempted to lighten the mood. "How do you know he has a furry ass?"

"I've seen his stupid butt naked more times than I can count," he growled—and I wasn't going to ask. Then his eyes focused on mine, and his lips landed hard on my mouth. This *corporate rich man* owned the kiss. He deflected and countered, dominating every move when I tried to take over. When he breathed, I breathed.

It was the best kiss of my life.

My moan was soft and fulfilled.

He pulled back, just to kiss my lips softly.

My lips curled in yearning. "I like that."

He hummed and nipped my bottom lip.

Not gently. And I liked that too.

Godric was a man of contradictions.

His hips pulled back and rammed into me hard enough that I jerked at the loud crash of the headboard. The wood holding it together had cracked somewhere. I was sure of that. With each thrust of his hips, his glorious cock sliding in my wet channel, the frame of the bed splintered. And it didn't stop him. Or me.

I ground against him just as hard as he slammed into me, each of us feeding on pleasure alone. My hands gripped his hair again and tugged his face back down to mine. And this time, I kissed the living shit out of him, our tongues rubbing just as scandalously as our bodies were.

The grooves of the headboard jabbed into my butt and my shoulder blades with each shove, and it only added to the delight of the hard sex he gave. I twirled my fingers in his hair and then yanked his head back in a sharp movement. He groaned in pleasure, the muscles in his neck showing in stark relief. I leaned forward and licked at them, tasting the sweat that glistened on his skin. Damn if he didn't taste just like he smelled—wild spice and cherries.

Godric growled low in his throat when I gently bit the side of his neck. "Do that again. Harder."

I sank my teeth in with a decent hold and released his hair to hug him close around his neck. He pounded into me more brutally, and I screamed against his skin. I released my bite to tip my head back and close my eyes, shouting, "Yes, yes, yes. Right there, Godric. Right there."

My hearing died a blissful death as I went over the edge and my hands flew up to the headboard to press my body harder against his. His fingers dug into my hips as my legs quivered against his sides, holding me steady for his continual onslaught of wild plunges. He was in complete control of my body as he dove into his own ecstasy, his roar against my shoulder the only sound I could hear floating in shocking heat as I was.

But he wasn't done. His cock remained hard inside of me even after coming with such force that I shivered in the afterglow. Godric pulled his cock out of my core and arranged me on my hands and knees in the center of his bed. With one of his forearms to my back, I lowered my shoulders to the mattress. He grabbed my hands and pulled them behind my back, holding both my small wrists in one of his hands. His other palm grabbed my shoulder right as he pushed his cock back into my still spasming core.

"Oh, fuck me," I babbled in pleasure.

"That's the plan," he said with a groan. He retreated and then shoved his hips back between my legs, his cock pressing like a dream inside my pussy. "I'm going to really fuck you now."

I tipped my forehead against the mattress staring down my body to his legs. "That wasn't fucking before?"

"I was being gentle."

I groaned. "Oh, fuck me."

"Yes, we've already gone over that."

Godric proceeded to show me just how gentle he had been before. With each new thrust of his hips, my shoulders slammed down into the bed. I opened my mouth and bit the comforter to muffle every scream of pleasure.

It didn't help.

I spat the material out, clenched my hands into fists inside his restraining hold, and chanted his name like he was a god. But I wasn't completely ashamed— his own chorus of shouts and roars boomed through the night right along with mine. With one smooth move, he tugged on my wrists, yanking my back up against his chest. The bed spun for a moment as dizziness took hold, but he released my wrists and gripped me around my waist with one muscled arm, his constant thrusts never ending.

Godric's fingers grazed my neck as he brushed my hair from my shoulder. His lips kissed and caressed from my ear down my sensitive neck, licking away my own sweat. He growled deep inside his chest, opened his mouth wide...

And he *bit* me.

His teeth sank into the soft spot between my neck and my shoulder. I bowed against his body, but his arm around my stomach rose, and he restrained my body effectively. My head fell back against his shoulder as I shouted in pained ecstasy, my mind shattering into the heavens as a climax hit so hard that I lost my breath.

Time...just gone. *Poof.*

Tiny blood drops trickled down my chest from his savage bite, and he came so furiously, I was sure the entire base heard his deep bellow. His cock pumped deep inside my channel, filling me once again with his heated cum. The body pressed against mine shook in the profound glory of carnal joy only mind-blowing sex affords.

As one, we slumped forward onto the mattress.

CHAPTER SIX

Godric's lips curved against my back. "You're still shaking."

The side of my damp face was smashed against his comforter. I mumbled, "So are you, big man."

He chuckled quietly, his accent so delicious. "Big man?"

"It's better than what you called me."

"Pet isn't bad." He opened his mouth and licked along my spine. "I like petting you."

His fingers fluttered over my ass and then lower until he was cupping my core. He rubbed softly back and forth to prove his point.

I moaned. "Okay. Pet is good."

The softest lips pressed against my shoulder as he spoke, muffling his words. "I thought so."

My eyes closed in giddiness when he touched my clit with a gentle finger. "Again?"

"Yes, again." His cock was already hard on my leg that he rested on. "Or are you too sore—"

His door swung open once more. Just a crack.

"Sir...," Jonathan muttered with exasperation from outside in the hallway. "You are now over an hour late to the meeting."

Godric groaned and banged his forehead against my back. He growled in protest. "That bastard made me wait."

"And now you've made him wait."

My lips trembled in humor.

Jonathan had some balls. Too furry or not.

"Fine. She needs to leave soon anyway," Godric groaned and licked up my spine again. "I'll be out in a minute."

Jonathan cleared his throat. "Thank you. I'm sure the men would like to go to bed at some point tonight."

Godric glanced up. "Jonathan."

Innocence spoke from afar. "Yes, sir?"

"Shut. The. Door."

The door shut—hard.

"Asshole," Godric muttered.

I rolled over under him and peered up into the most striking eyes. I smiled with true delight. "Well, big man, it's been fun."

"It has." His head tilted and his tawny curls ran over his shoulder. "I'd like to see you again. Would you consider taking a vacation to New City soon? I could come here, but it would be with all the guards."

I lifted my left hand and ran the pads of my fingers over his shoulder, his tan skin like silk, absently twirling his hair around my fingers. After a moment of thought, I decided to tell the truth.

"I'm going to New City tonight."

He was corporate. That was where the top corporations were headquartered. Essentially, I was telling him that I wouldn't mind seeing him again, too. This test drive had been a success in my book.

His brows rose, but he didn't comment on my destination. He merely lifted my arm with my silver bracelet and touched his bracelet against mine, stating loudly for his device, "Order: exchange number. Name: Poppy Bree."

Golden eyes flicked to mine, waiting for me.

I paused a second, making him wait before I spoke loudly, "Order: exchange number. Name: Godric Leon."

Our bracelets shone white for a moment, the information transferring. We lowered our arms when it was done, the glow diminished.

Godric leaned down and kissed my cheek with soft lips and brushed his fingers gently over the bruises on my wrists caused by his earlier restraining hold, a tender but silent apology. Then he shoved off the bed and grabbed his suit pants from the floor. I rolled on my side and watched as he stuffed his legs into them, zipping and buttoning.

He marched to the door and glanced at me. The man didn't put on a shirt or shoes. Just his pants, his toes even showing. With his hair still askew from my fingers, he flicked a finger at me. "Cover up."

I raised a brow at the demand, but I had already been grabbing for the edge of the blanket. I wasn't keen on his entire guard seeing me naked and freshly fucked. I tucked it over my shoulder and dug my feet down into the soft blanket.

He finally nodded, done evaluating that I was covered to his liking. Silly man. If we were going to see each other at a later date, he would learn that I didn't take orders all that well. That only worked in the bedroom with long bouts of sex included.

With his right hand on the doorknob, he stated, "I'll leave a few guards outside the door for you. They'll make sure you make it to your quarters safely."

I opened my mouth to argue, but he had already turned away and slipped out the door. I hadn't even needed to cover up. The man had skated out, barely opening the door.

Jonathan grumbled, "You can't be serious, sir."

"It's the middle of the night. If he can dare to make me wait this long, then he can see me straight out of bed," Godric disputed with heat, his tone business-pissed. He swiftly shut the door behind him, blocking out any further argument between the two.

I stretched underneath the blanket and debated taking a quick nap, but with a glimpse at the clock— almost two o'clock in the morning—I decided against it. My train was leaving at four, only two hours away.

I groaned as I rolled out of bed, my body aching in all the wonderful places it should after a delectable night with a man who knew what he was doing.

I dressed and entered the bathroom to use the facilities. But my reflection gave me pause in the mirror. My white t-shirt was stained red in sporadic blotches near my neck. I pulled it away carefully to examine the damage.

My nose scrunched at the view.

Godric had really bitten me.

It was probably going to scar where each of his blunt teeth had sunk in. I groaned and used a washcloth to delicately dab away any remaining blood. But my shirt was no good. Any of the personnel here would take notice and inform my father. That would not be wise with my current plans.

I exited the bathroom and examined the plush bedroom. I had been in this one before, escaping to these rooms from time to time for solitude. I knew the VIP section just as well as I knew my own. And since Godric had ruined my shirt, he now owed me one.

I rifled through his luggage and found a gray sweater that wouldn't catch anyone's attention. I pulled it on over my head and pushed the sleeves up on my arms. It was big, but I occasionally wore my clothing large for comfort.

The weapon he had left caught my attention as I stuffed my hair up into my ball cap. My eyes flew over the weird object. There was a black handle, and then it curved in a ninety-degree angle with a silver barrel that was the same length as the handle. His warning 'not to touch' didn't bother me. I picked it up gently from the bedside table and turned it over in my hands. It was heavier than a knife.

I lifted the end of the barrel close to my right eye and shut my left. But I couldn't see anything down the small hole. There was no blade inside it. I sniffed at it, but there wasn't a smell, no poisons inside. My brows furrowed as I sat it back down.

No wonder he'd left it behind. It was useless.

I shook my head and walked to the door, picking up my own blades and strapping them to my legs as I went. Now, these were good weapons. Anyone who wanted to stay alive in this broken section of the world knew how to use a knife. If you had the money to train, you would know how to use a sword. And if you had even more money to train with the best around the world, you didn't use any weapons. Your hands and feet would work just fine to subdue an attacker—or more.

I peeked through the peephole of the door.

The four guards Godric had left behind definitely had pretty and deadly swords, just like the others had. The metal blades gleamed under the lighting outside, allowing me to see them easily in their black uniforms. I stepped away from the door.

I couldn't go that way.

They couldn't follow me.

The only other way out was a tight squeeze. But I was little. I wiggled my shoulders and went back into the bathroom and straight to the toilet. There was a small break in the wall where the corners met. I ran my fingers along it until I found the hidden latch. The housekeepers would use these hidden doors back before the base upgraded with electronic entry doors. Visitors were always losing their keys back then.

I slipped into the small hidden walkway and shut the hidden door without a squeak. I paid attention to where I was walking in the complete darkness, afraid I would trip. It was my head that jarred back when I rammed into a small area where the ceiling dipped down.

"Dammit." I rubbed at my forehead.

After three minutes of walking in pitch black, I placed my right hand on the wall and slowed my pace. I was far enough away now that Godric's guards would be a few hallways over. The tips of my fingers brushed dust until they dipped the smallest bit into the wall.

I stopped and turned, walking my hands up and down the wall until I found another latch. With a little muscle, I pulled the door open and snuck inside silently. I listened in the dark of a different bathroom.

The room was empty, no VIPs in this one.

I grinned and shut the hidden door as I strolled out of the quarters with no guards to follow me. Success.

CHAPTER SEVEN

I yawned behind a fist while making my way through the base. I'd walked the halls of the VIP area without seeing any of the Liberated Army, my father's foot soldiers. There were many bases all over the world for the LA, but this was the home base for their General—and me, his child.

The main section came up quickly, and I checked my bracelet again. I'd only wasted twenty minutes eluding Godric's guards in the hidden passageways. I had plenty of time to take a shower before leaving the base.

I lifted my head to watch where I was walking, lest I fall on my face, which had occurred more times than I liked to admit. My steps faltered though when I saw what was straight ahead a few more feet. It was a conference room my father typically used to intimidate, where plenty of LA soldiers walked by in their menacing red uniforms, showcasing the power my father had.

I stopped completely when I saw who was inside.

My father was there, and he had taken notice of me through the glass barrier. He had twenty soldiers lined up along the walls on his side of the table, and a few others were sitting next to him.

But on the other side of the room was Godric, leaning back in a conference room chair with his legs spread wide while he spoke to my father. His guards, dressed all in black, were positioned against the walls at his end of the table. He had no one sitting next to him, conducting the meeting by himself.

I looked right to a hallway I could sneak off to—but my father flicked a hidden hand, indicating he wanted me to come into the room.

My eyes widened.

My father never wanted me in his meetings.

I swallowed down my nervousness.

There was no way he could know my plans.

Or who I had been with tonight.

I hesitated when Godric stretched his neck and paused as he saw me standing outside the room. Maybe my father did know. There were cameras on base.

I wiggled the bill of my ball cap down and shoved my shoulders back. There was only one way to find out why he wanted me in there. So I walked forward with fabricated ease, keeping my attention on the door.

Godric's brows furrowed as he scanned the area behind me, and he placed his hands on the armrests of his chair. He started to stand. But he ever so slowly sat back down, calm and casual, when he noticed my father already standing up with his attention on me.

My father arrived at the door before me and opened it, allowing me entry. All the guards on my father's side took one glance at me and looked away, their attention back on Godric's guards. And Godric's guards peered in my direction, then away...and quickly back again when they realized it was me—the woman who had fucked their boss less than a half hour ago.

My father indicated for me to follow him.

I peeked at Godric's face, but all confusion had cleared from his features. He now wore a bored expression—though his golden eyes were watching with patient intelligence. He had to be wondering why the hell I was here and why the great General Carvene seemed to want me here.

My father glanced in Godric's direction, glaring with cool eyes. "Excuse me a moment. There's someone I'd like Poppy to meet."

"What?" I asked, utterly confused.

Godric raised a brow. "Who exactly is this woman to interrupt our meeting?" He flicked a finger at me. "This is highly unorthodox."

My father snapped, "And so is your attire."

Godric's lips curved at the edges, enjoying my father's anger. "You didn't answer my question, General Carvene."

My father ground his teeth together, glancing back at his side of the table before he pressed his hand to my back guiding me in Godric's direction. I pushed against his palm, digging in my feet, but my father only pressed harder. I breathed in through my nose deeply, trying not to hyperventilate the closer we got.

Godric's brows rose, but he stood calmly to his feet.

We stopped directly in front of his bare chest.

My father kept his hand on my back and gestured to Godric with his free one. "Poppy, this is Mr. King." His hand waved in my direction. "Mr. King, this is my daughter, Poppy."

My jaw dropped an inch.

Godric's jaw ground together.

Our eyes held one another's.

One of his guards coughed in the silence, a hacking cough that had a few of my father's men turning their gazes in his direction.

But not my father's.

Not mine.

Not Godric's.

My father glanced back and forth between us, his brows furrowing as he stopped staring at me. "Poppy..."

I shook my head and instantly stuck out my hand. "It's nice to meet you, *Mr. King*." My nostrils gradually flared in a fury. "I hope your stay here so far has been pleasant."

Another cough from Godric's bodyguard. Same guy.

Godric popped his neck and placed his hand in mine. "It's lovely to meet you too, *Ms. Carvene*." He dipped and kissed the top of my hand and then glared up at me. "And, yes, my stay has been amenable thus far."

I jerked my hand away from him, crossing my arms over my chest as he straightened to his intimidating height.

Godric tilted his head. "Poppy is an interesting name."

"I guess so." I shrugged. "My middle name is Bree. Poppy Bree Carvene."

He rubbed absently at his chest—his very bare chest—as he continued to stare at me through thin slits of his eyes. "Lovely name. Mine is Godric Leon King."

I shrugged again, looking away from him.

Mr. King was my father's sworn enemy.

CHAPTER EIGHT

My father grunted, muttering under his breath, "That's about how I thought the introduction would go."

I glared at him. "Why did you want me in here?"

Godric muttered just as quietly as my father had, "Because he's an overbearing ass."

I flayed him with a death stare.

My father chose to ignore Godric's comment, and motioned down the table, flicking his wrist. "Poppy, someone arrived in time for this meeting. Because it was late." He managed to snub Godric—or so he thought.

I swiftly understood my father had no clue why the meeting was derailed. Oh, like his only daughter having sex with the richest man in the world, the man who ran every single corporation on this fucking planet. The man who battled with him constantly on the Liberated Army's involvement with restoring our world to working order, not just what the corporations deemed as law.

And the corporations were the law.

If the LA hadn't been formed years ago and had such a wide span hold on the world's remaining population, Godric would have crushed them instantly. Now he just did it over time.

One base gone over two years?

No one notices.

One hundred bases gone in an instant?

Godric would have an uprising.

He was intelligent, feared, wealthy, and owned the Corporate Army to do his blood work if needed. It had also been said he did his own dirty jobs when he was bored.

Bored of...ruling the world.

An egotistical ass wasn't a strong enough name for what he was. His power knew no bounds. And he relished it.

I could see that now in the way he stood, how he didn't give a shit how he dressed for his most prominent adversary. The man knew he couldn't be toppled.

My father flicked his wrist again, his attention still down the table on his side of the room. "Brandon, I'd like you to officially meet my daughter."

I sneered once more at Godric.

He merely raised a brow, but he was still scowling.

I turned slightly, not giving him my back, but looked to where my father was indicating. A man stood from his chair, his gaze on mine. He walked with a steady gait in our direction, his eyes never leaving mine. His hair was raven black and his eyes a piercing green. He was at least a foot taller than me, and his red uniform fit his muscled form with care. His features were rugged, yet refined in a cultured money way.

Brandon was simply breathtaking to look at.

I glanced back to my father, confusion written all over my features. "Father?"

He had been watching my reaction, and a silly grin lifted his features in pleasure. "Poppy, this is Brandon Moore." He peered to the newcomer. "Brandon, this is my daughter, Poppy Carvene."

I lifted my hand to him. "It's nice to meet you."

"It's wonderful to meet you too, Ms. Carvene. Your father has told me all about you." He bent and kissed my hand. His lips lingered a second too long.

I blushed at the action and gradually took my hand back as he stood straight. I had to blink a few times before I jerked my head to my father, a silent question in my eyes.

My father still had that stupid smile on his face. He tipped his head in Brandon's direction, keeping his gaze on mine, entirely too pleased with himself for some reason.

"Poppy, this is Brandon. Your fiancé." And my father freaking winked. "I told you that you'd like him."

All expression cleared from my features.

I sucked in a harsh breath.

My head snapped back to...my fiancé.

Then back to my father.

"Oh, my God," I muttered.

Godric's bodyguard started coughing again.

CHAPTER NINE

My father's smile faltered. "Poppy, are you okay?"

This just wasn't right. I couldn't breathe.

I glanced at Brandon again.

His green gaze didn't miss anything. "It is late, General Carvene." He turned his striking regard to my father. "Perhaps we can save any further discussions with Ms. Carvene until tomorrow morning? This is a lot for her to take in without sleep."

I nodded enthusiastically, unable to speak.

I needed to get the fuck out of here.

A train waited with my name on it.

My father touched my cheek. "What are you doing up so late?"

I croaked, "I went for a walk. I was restless."

He nodded his head and lowered his hand from my face. "That's understandable." He turned to Brandon, his smile back in full force. "She knew you were coming tomorrow."

Godric lifted his left hand and studied his nails.

The situation was truly messed up.

Godric picked at his pinky nail—there was nothing wrong with it—and peered over his shoulder, not a smidge of emotion on his features. Bored.

"Jonathan, why don't you get some water for that cough." It was an order.

The coughing guard was Jonathan. White haired and broad shouldered. Damn beautiful in his black uniform as he walked past me and out the door, not arguing with Godric this time. Completely professional.

I motioned with my thumb behind me. "I'm going to head to our quarters, Father."

He nodded. "I'll be here. I don't think this meeting will end anytime soon."

I nodded in agreement and turned to my fiancé. I made myself speak the words in a calm fashion and lifted my hand in his direction again. "Mr. Moore, it was nice meeting you."

He tipped down and kissed the top of my hand again, once more lingering too long—as if he had the right to kiss me. An agreement on paper did not give him that right, not in my opinion. "The pleasure was all mine, Ms. Carvene."

My chest rose as I inhaled deeply and turned the other way. I raised my hand again. "Mr. King." I didn't say it was nice meeting him.

The right side of Godric's lips tipped up in a cocky and sexy smirk, and he bowed over my hand and took it in his own. "It was a pleasure, Ms. Carvene."

When he kissed the top of my hand, his thumb slid beneath the sweater that had rolled down my arms, hiding my bruised wrists. He pressed hard on the bruise—right at my pulse point.

I didn't flinch but merely held his stare as he straightened. Asshole. He hadn't liked my brush-off and told me so in his own way.

I turned to the door, walking toward it.

But I pivoted and marched back to my father.

I tossed my arms around his neck, hugging him close.

He grunted in surprise but quickly enfolded me in his arms. The General wasn't the best with affection, but he had never denied me a hug. He patted my back and waited until I let go to lower his arms.

His brows rose when I stepped back.

I shrugged. "I love you, Father."

He blinked. "Poppy, are you really all right?"

"I'm fine. I'm fine. I just wanted a hug before I went to bed." Before I left you for New City. "That's all, Father."

He nodded his head, but concern still shone in his eyes. "Well, goodnight. And I love you too."

With one last look at him, I left the room.

* * *

Jonathan was trailing me. And there was no damn water in his hands. Godric had sent him outside to follow my whereabouts. He was quickly catching up with me, no longer 'hiding' the closer I got to my quarters.

I rounded the last corner and walked faster. The LA guards were just at the end. Only authorized personnel were allowed past that point. I glanced behind me and picked up my pace even more.

Jonathan's eyes narrowed on the guards, and he began running. He lifted his right arm. "Ms. Carvene! Wait just a moment."

To hell with that.

The look in his eyes was not of peace talking.

I sprinted to the end of the hallway.

The guards let me through instantly.

The whisper of swords being drawn echoed behind me. My father's soldiers took offense seeing a Corporate Army guard chasing after me.

Right before I rushed into my quarters, I peered over my right shoulder. Jonathan had his hands up in the air, not fighting with the guards as they questioned him, but he glared daggers in my direction. I quickly shut my door behind me, locking it with a simple command.

I grabbed my bag out of my room, no time for a shower now with my father's interference. I pulled the tablet from the side of my bag, and left it near the refrigerator. It was for my father. He would find it tomorrow when he woke, my reason for leaving clearly written on the screen.

I ambled around our cozy quarters, touching objects that were memories to me. I pulled my ball cap lower over my suddenly wet and burning eyes, and whispered, "Goodbye, Father."

I left through the back exit.

I had a train to catch.

CHAPTER TEN

I tipped my head down against the whipping wind that blew dust into my eyes. The pavement was cracked with grass growing in sporadic spots in this part of the decimated old city. History books explained it was once called Norfolk, Virginia. The new world called it Port because of its easy access to the harbors on the Atlantic Ocean for shipping goods around the world. Occasional storms would hammer the docks, but Port was still the largest city for shipping in the King Western Province—ruled by none other than Godric.

Certain territories in the world still didn't have a designation after stupid ass people tore our planet apart. War had been a powerful and destructive tool a hundred and fifty years ago. The King Western Province included the entire continent of North America. South America was still dark, only renegades and criminals living there. However, from what my father expressed recently, Mr. King—Godric—was readying his troops to change that soon with the influence and money of the corporations backing him.

I jogged down another demolished street with my bag slapping against my right side. The prime sectors of Port, near the Liberated Army's base, were new and pristine. This section wasn't one of them. I regulated my breathing and kept my head down in case a drone flew by searching the area for lawbreakers.

My train wasn't in the common district of Port's

transport dockyards. My father knew all the mainstream trains leaving from those docks. I couldn't take the chance of one of his soldiers catching me there, either. They all knew me. So most of my savings I spent on securing discrete transportation to New City, a train my father would never find.

The leaves on the trees growing up through the destroyed houses rustled as the wind picked up; the scent of salt lingered in the air. The ride to New City would be bumpy if the wind continued to batter the shoreline. I was not excited to travel alone on the ocean, but the train ride would afford my weary body a few hours of sleep.

I stopped behind a rusted red truck with no tires or doors and sat down on the concrete pebbles and bits of sand. The breeze quieted, but the waves of the ocean nearby were loud. I listened closely in the murkiness as I waited for my contact.

An animal nearby lurked, his silver eyes staring from his crouched position in the shadows of stacked debris. The animal was slight, but I knew better than to test boundaries with the wildlife. They could be rabid, and then you were dead if you scuffled with them. Many had died a gruesome death by contracting rabies from an animal they thought sweet and defenseless.

A shooting star traced the night sky.

"I wish my ride would hurry the hell up," I grumbled, keeping a suspicious eye on the critter.

A skittering on the pavement to my left.

My muscles tensed.

Then a sheep ambled in front of me in the dark.

It didn't look my way as it carefully chose where to place its cloven hooves on the cracked concrete. The white fur was gray with dust, and an old scar ran down its ribs. One leg had fresh blood trailing down its fur from a gruesome cut.

The animal hidden in the debris didn't even turn its silver eyes to the easy target. It kept watching me.

I was the better meal, apparently.

A low whistle eventually captured my attention.

I squinted to the right, only the full moon above veiled by the rolling cloud cover.

Two blinks of light on the beach.

My ride was here.

CHAPTER ELEVEN

Half my attention rested on the lurking animal and the other half on my contact. He was short and stout, his scruffy beard dark brown. I knew his head was bald, but tonight he wore a stocking cap over his skin to fight against the chill in the air. When I was far enough away from the stalking eyes of the animal, I turned completely on the sand and waved.

I called, "Hi, James. Thank you for coming on short notice."

He smiled in greeting, showing his missing front tooth. "Anything for you, Poppy."

I'd been there the day he lost his tooth. It wasn't from a fight. Instead, he was kicked in the face by a horse, knocking him out completely. I still didn't know why he had been trying to wrangle the beast to ride it. But my best guess was a bet made with his friends. He would do anything for money.

I pointed to the single train cabin silently hovering over the sand. "Are you sure this will make it to New City?"

The transport wasn't new, but the blue, clean energy glowing from underneath the metal slats was steady. It kept the train afloat without wavering as the wind gusted again. I still found it humorous that the corporations had modeled our most common mode of transportation after ancient trains—like the kind of transport that had actually run on rails when the world was once beautiful. It was odd and symbolic of days past when the corporations only looked to the future.

James thumped me on my shoulder. "I wouldn't put you in danger. This will get you there in plenty of time for your sign up at the Military House."

I rubbed the shoulder he'd smacked. It was my injured one. "I really can't thank you enough."

His smile was sweet. "Never fear. James is always here to rescue a beautiful woman."

I snorted and lifted my silver bracelet. "And to take her money."

"That too." He pressed his bracelet against mine.

I stated loudly, "Order: Transfer two thousand units. Name: James Bartell."

"Order: Accept two thousand units. Name: Poppy Carvene."

Our bracelets glowed white in the night before we lowered our arms. My side of the bargain was complete.

James checked his bracelet and nodded. "The transfer is good." He swung his hand to the train. "She's all yours for a one-way passage."

I hesitated, staring at the transport. "Do I need to do anything?" Soldiers always took care of my needs. This was a new experience for me.

He chuckled and shook his head. "No. I've already programmed the destination in." He nudged his shoulder with mine. "Go get 'em, Poppy. Make me proud."

I turned and hugged him. "Thank you so much."

He released me and wiggled the bill of my ball cap. "Don't be nervous."

"I'm not." I straightened up fast.

He waved his hand to the waiting train.

My sneakers dug into the sand as I walked to the black metal stairs, the door already open. When I was at the top of them, I peered back.

"James, remember, my father will probably

question you. Tell him I made you do this."

His smile was amused, staring up at me from the beach. "And he'll believe it too. Anyone who knows you would believe it." He waved. "You'll do just fine. I promise."

I sucked in a large lungful of salty sea air and then stepped inside the train. The door was heavy to close, but it locked simply enough with a command. I waited only a second before stating, "Go."

The only indication the train had started to move was the vibration of clean energy thrumming with heavy force under my feet. I lifted the blind covering the lone window and peered outside. The moon sparkled on the ocean's surface thirty feet below as the train moved over the water.

I dropped my bag on one of the two chairs and grinned at the sandwich on the other seat. James had left me a treat. I pounced on the nourishment and moved behind the seats to the small, simple bed resting against the back wall. The only other part of the cabin was a lone bathroom at the front.

The cushion of the bed sunk only an inch when I sat down. It wasn't the swankiest transport I'd ever been in, but it was the only one I had ever paid for myself. I started to bite into the sandwich but stalled, my hands halfway to my mouth.

A small head of silver fur poked out from underneath the seat on the left. Silver eyes stared up at my face and silently evaluated my person. Cute pointed ears twitched as I held perfectly still.

It was a fox.

The creature that had been stalking me on the beach had snuck onboard. And this train didn't stop. Or, at least, I had no freaking clue how to turn it around.

I breathed evenly, searching its eyes for any sign of attack. I was stuck with the little beast until New City—more than five hours away.

I swallowed, and whispered, "Um...hello there."

The ears twitched again.

Its eyes glanced at my sandwich.

My mouth bobbed. If it wanted my food instead of my arm to gnaw on, I was all for that. "Are you hungry?"

The animal kept his belly on the ground, dragging itself carefully out from under the seat. It peered at my sandwich again, and its tongue lolled outside its mouth.

I think it was smiling.

"All right." I tore a piece of turkey off and tossed it down on the floor. "Try that."

The fox stood up and ducked its head to sniff at the meat. It was a male with strong muscles under its coat. The little beast didn't appear to be starving like most wildlife, his silver fur healthy and shining in the light.

He ate the turkey in one bite.

I tossed him another piece.

He caught it in the air and swallowed it whole.

Then he jumped onto the bed.

I skittered to a stand.

But all he did was trot to the end of the bed and lay down, curling his tail around himself. Then he closed his eyes. His breathing evened out...as he fell asleep.

"Okay, okay," I muttered in shock.

The fox was healthy. He just wanted a nap.

I sat down carefully on the bed.

He didn't move.

The sandwich smelled delicious, so I quickly took a bite and watched the fox for any indication that he was going to pounce. The little beast never even twitched. I eventually ate the rest of my sandwich and licked my fingers clean.

He still didn't move, only his chest expanding with each easy breath he took as he slept on peacefully.

The thin mattress creaked as I attempted to

situate myself on the bed, leaving the fox plenty of room below my feet. I rested my head down on my arms that I had tucked under my head, lying on my side pressed against the back wall. As an afterthought, I pulled one of my blades from its sheath on my thigh and held it close as I closed my eyes.

CHAPTER TWELVE

The dinging bell of the train woke me.

I tipped my head up and yawned. There was light streaming in through the window—a lot of light. It was mid-afternoon by the blinding sun pouring inside the cabin.

I had arrived in New City.

Or what history books used to call Lisbon, Portugal.

Either way, it was now part of King Central Province.

The fox was sitting patiently at the door.

I snorted and stuffed my blade away. "I take it you're ready to get off this fun filled ride?"

His tongue lolled out, another grin.

I glanced at my bracelet.

I had overslept an hour. I only had two hours remaining before I needed to be at the Military House. At five o'clock in the evening, the Corporate Army shut their doors, no more entries for another six months. I would be too old then to enter—only ages eighteen to twenty-four allowed to sign up. I was turning twenty-five in two weeks. This was my official last shot to scrap an arranged marriage—the only way it could be done for a female.

There was one problem.

I didn't have a clue where the Military House was.

Out of all the cities I had visited in my life, New

City wasn't one of them. My father avoided this place like it was haunted by demons. And, to him, people who worked for the corporations were demons.

I grabbed my bag, put the strap over my shoulder, and unlocked the door to the train. As soon as I opened the train's door, the bustle of a thriving city attacked my senses. The clamor was more overwhelming than any city I knew.

The sun instantly warmed my neck while I stepped outside and walked down the stairs. I lifted my right hand to shield my eyes, even though the bill of my ball cap should have provided enough shading. Bright light still shimmered in my eyes, and I squinted and attempted to find the cause.

People strode by briskly, talking in groups or through their bracelets with little buds in their ears for privacy. I leaned to the left past an extremely tall man. My brows rose in shock at the view. There was an immense building that towered over all the structures, the very top of it with a curved decorative golden roof—a crown sitting atop the white skyscraper.

The sun reflecting off it burned my eyes.

"Good grief," I muttered.

The fox sat down next to my feet and panted.

This place was unbelievable.

Ego and wealth even poured off the residents, their clothes made of the finest material, and their faces painted in makeup I had never been interested in wearing. Their attire was similar to the sweater I still wore of Godric's, the stitching twice as nice and delectably softer than any soldier's clothing in Port. It was a miracle my father hadn't noticed the difference in my typical sweaters versus this one, now that I really thought about it.

"Where the hell do I go now?" I mumbled.

The port in New City was outrageously busy today.

I lifted a hand to an elderly woman walking by, her red hat sporting a purple feather. "Excuse me, ma'am. Do you know how to get to the Military House?"

She glanced up and down my person in a slow perusal. Then she sniffed in my direction and walked right past me without helping. The feather in her hat even tilted away from me in the salty breeze.

At least that wasn't any different from other cities.

Newcomers weren't shunned, but they weren't welcomed with opened arms either. Protection and suspicion kept most residents in tight familiar groups. Anyone who didn't know where they were going inside your city was definitely not familiar.

"I guess I'll have to do this the hard way." I peered down at the fox that stood close but didn't touch. "I doubt you'll be welcome here."

He showed a little of his sharp teeth.

I shrugged. "I'm not even welcome here."

The fox whined, his head tilting back with it.

"I'm sorry." I shooed him with both hands. "Go on now. You don't want someone slitting your throat just to have a nice silver fur hat."

As if he understood me, he jerked his adorable head in the direction the snobbish woman had disappeared. He raced away, his furry tail swooshing back and forth.

My companion on this trip was now gone.

I was truly alone.

CHAPTER THIRTEEN

"Please just tell me where the Military House is," I begged.

Yet another resident of New City lifted their nose in my direction and passed me by. The streets were crowded, and the buildings were too polished. I'd literally had to buy a pair of sunglasses. All of the sparkling windows and gleaming metals and coppers were hard to view. I was used to the concrete coloring of the military bases around the world. My eyes couldn't handle all of the vibrant colors at once, each new turn down a different street startling with a kaleidoscope of brilliant shades of the rainbow.

And it was so *shiny*.

I groaned and rubbed my forehead. I stood frozen on the sidewalk of another street of visual pain and peered left and right. No one was going to speak with me.

I was running out of time!

I only had fifteen minutes left.

I wished again for the hundredth time since entering this godforsaken city that the Military House had a number listed in a directory. Any directory. I had checked them all when buying my sunglasses.

I stretched my back muscles and started running.

Ten minutes later, I stopped to take a breath.

My hands were on my sides while my chest heaved with much-needed oxygen. Sweat beaded down my temples and under my heavy sweater. I dropped my bag for relief from the weight while I searched frantically for any indication of where I was supposed to be.

I had stopped directly in front of the ginormous building that wore a golden crown. This street was even more blinding because of the damn thing. I turned and glared at the white monstrosity.

Then I read the lettering on the massive sign in the sloping courtyard of grass. Fucking unbelievable.

It was King Corporation.

I couldn't get away from the man.

The man who put a damn crown on his building.

He couldn't be any more arrogant if he wanted.

A group of men sauntered by, all tall and fit. They held coffee cups in their hands and sipped the hot liquid with leisure as they chatted together. They wore simple dress slacks and collared shirts. But all ten men paused in their trek in the courtyard where they were heading to King Corporation. As one, they straightened and turned around, scanning the area with their laser focus.

I glanced around for signs of fighting.

Except no trouble was happening.

There were only more innocent people in their flashy attire walking toward their destinations, a few with swords strapped to their back or hips and others with knives like mine. It was all very normal.

The group of men kept glancing side to side.

I hesitated but grabbed my bag and hurried in their direction. Ten people to ask were better than one on the street.

The guy in the middle muttered, "I didn't think he was coming back until tomorrow. I still need to get that project done. I figured I had another day."

They all appeared confused, still searching.

"Maybe he returned early," another guy mumbled.

"Excuse me!" I stated, still out of breath. I waved

my hand and caught their attention. When they didn't instantly ignore me like half the people in New City did, I moved even faster. I stopped directly in front of them, and asked quickly, "Do any of you know where the Military House is?"

All ten men froze where they stood.

My red brows puckered.

They were going to ignore me too. I just knew it.

"Please," I begged. My head was tilted all the way back to stare into their eyes. They were damn big. "I only have a few minutes before I need to be there. Will you please help me?"

The man in the middle coughed behind a quick fist and stared hard at me. "Where did you say, miss?"

My eyes widened in delight. Those were more words than anyone had spoken to me all day. I rushed to speak, babbling, "The Military House. I only have a few minutes remaining before they lock their doors."

He blinked at me, inhaling deeply. His gaze ran over my features, his own eyes wide—but it looked like shock. "We can escort you there. It's just a street over."

"Yes!" I grabbed his hand and yanked him behind me, already walking over the soft hills of grass to the sidewalk. "Do you mind if we run?"

"Not at all, miss." When I released his hand, he started jogging just a little in front of me. He peered back over his shoulder. "Is this a good pace for you?"

"It's fine. Please just get me there."

There were pounding feet behind me.

I sucked oxygen at the quick run but glimpsed the glass of the building next to me. In the reflection, the other nine men were running behind me at a steady pace. It was extremely odd, but these men were my current saving grace—as long as they actually took me to the right place. Though, I was impressed none of them spilled their coffee while they ran. Their cups didn't have lids. My hand would have been burned all over if I were doing that.

They had been right. It was one street over

directly behind King Corporation. The golden crown even shaded a portion of the building at this time of day.

I stopped in front of a black, wrought iron fence.

There were spikes at the top of the fence, and the building was made of dark wood and rough stone. It was completely out of place next to the beauty surrounding it. It looked hundreds of years old with its turrets on each end, like an ancient castle, except for the embellished, fancy sign on the front that stated Military House.

The gate and front doors were still open.

I quickly shook the man's hand who had led the way here. "Thank you so very much."

He still wore a shocked expression, his mouth hanging open—and not because he was winded. "You're most welcome."

I nodded once to the others who had followed, and then I bolted through the front gate and ran up the walkway.

One of the men's voices carried quietly, "I would never have imagined that."

"It's been what? Over a hundred years..."

"I know."

I ignored whatever they were blathering on about and sprinted up the stairs. I stopped inside the doors where an older graying man in a Corporate Army uniform stood. I placed my hands on my knees and panted.

I whispered in awe, "I made it."

The CA soldier cleared his throat.

I stood up and placed my hands on my lower back, stretching my muscles. I removed my sunglasses and peeked up at him. "I'm here for the Corporate Army sign ups."

His gaze was cold as he looked me up and down. "Are you sure, miss?" He glanced at his silver bracelet, checking the time.

That was a better response than I had received

from other CA soldiers when I had stopped them to ask for directions. Those assholes had taken one look at my smaller stature and just laughed at me.

I nodded. "I'm sure."

"Then you made it just in time."

He shut and locked the heavy wooden doors.

CHAPTER FOURTEEN

The dining hall was filled with a little over one hundred candidates. Only ten of those were women. They had already sent home seventy-four others who didn't have the right forms filled out or were missing signatures from a male legal guardian. The meal we were eating wasn't terrible as I had feared. It had all the basic food groups.

The worst part was waiting for a CA soldier to come into the room and call out one of our names. They could do it anytime, and we would then leave for an interview. Most already had theirs completed, having arrived days earlier. Only a few candidates arrived today as I had, and the interviews were running nonstop. My turn was coming soon.

The two girls on either side of me ate silently. No female was here to make friends. It was common knowledge that only twenty percent of the women passed the requirements to become a CA soldier. So that meant only two out of the ten of us would obtain a position within the Corporate Army. The other eight would leave to become breeding machines for a husband.

I chewed the corn on my plate, trying to enjoy the scrumptious vegetable. I wasn't hungry, but I knew I would need the energy. Plus, I didn't have a lot of units remaining to spend. My sunglasses had cost more than five expensive meals in Port. New City was expensive.

The door opened, and the room quieted.

A soldier in black stated loudly, "Poppy Carvene."

All eyes inside the room suddenly went on alert, more than a few gasps were heard. My father was legendary. And so was his hatred for anything corporate—especially for Mr. King who ran it all. The other candidates' reactions weren't surprising.

"Poppy Carvene," the soldier repeated.

I lowered my fork and stood.

I kept my shoulders back and my gaze straight.

The eyes spearing me with curiosity were mostly annoying, though my cheeks blushed in shame. Word would soon get out that General Carvene's only child didn't agree with his politics. This would hurt him in some circles.

He was tough, though.

My father hadn't held his position for over thirty years without knowing how to deal with problems such as this. There had been many men who had tried to usurp him only to be burned down. Sometimes literally.

His contacts were endless.

I followed the soldier out of the room, thankful when he shut the door to the dining hall behind us, effectively cutting off the gossip murmuring through the crowd.

The soldier peered at me from the corner of his eye while leading me down a hallway to the back. "You're really General Carvene's daughter?"

I ground my teeth together. "I am."

He grunted and turned his eyes forward. "You won't have it easy here during the tests. Those recruits will be brutal."

"Because of who I am," I clarified.

"Yes."

"I know."

His eyes flicked to me once more, glancing down my body. "Do you think you have a chance?"

"I wouldn't be here if I didn't."

He chuckled. "Spoken like a general's child."

"Meaning?"

He stopped and opened a door for me. "Don't let your pride get in your way."

I stepped into the room and stared back at him.

I didn't have a superiority complex. Not at all.

He didn't enter the room with me. "Good luck."

He shut the door, the wood only inches from my nose.

"Ms. Poppy Carvene?" a woman asked from behind me.

I quickly twisted and wiped away any surprise.

The room wasn't empty.

Five CA soldiers were sitting at the back of the rectangular room. There was a long table in front of them with tablets for each person, and a lone chair sat facing their group. The room was white. Completely white, including the furniture.

Interview time.

I nodded and walked forward to the empty chair. "Yes, I'm Ms. Carvene."

Four men and one woman ran their intelligent eyes over my person. I hadn't had time to shower or change before the dinner bell had rung. I'd barely been assigned my small room and dropped off my bag before the herd of candidates had filled the housing hallways, all in a rush for the dining hall.

The woman gestured to the seat with a wave of her hand. "You may sit down."

"Thank you, ma'am." I sat and tried not to fidget.

She ran her fingers over her tablet, her piercing eyes lowering to the screen. "You're our last interview, so you're catching us at a great moment."

I breathed a sigh of relief.

The men didn't speak.

It looked like the woman was running this.

"I'll be honest with you, Ms. Carvene. I'm surprised your father signed off on your form." Her dark gaze flicked up to my brown eyes. "You do know that we will verify all signatures, correct?"

I blinked. "Yes."

I actually hadn't.

But if he read my letter, he knew where I was.

There was a ten-year minimum jail sentence for anyone who forged a legal guardian's name for entrance to the Corporate Army. I didn't think my father would tell them he hadn't actually signed it. I was twisting his arm, but it was needed for my freedom. I would apologize later.

I placed my hands on my lap and waited.

She continued to watch my every move. "Why do you want to join the Corporate Army?"

I nibbled on my bottom lip.

Her brows rose in the silence.

The truth was best here. "I don't want to marry a stranger. I don't want to be a parent right now. I want to run my own life."

The soldier blinked. "Thank you for your honesty."

I tipped my head in acknowledgment.

"Do you believe that you'll pass the tests here?"

"I do."

"What are your skills? Typically, women your size don't stand a chance here. But seeing as your father is General Carvene, I imagine he had you professionally trained?"

"Yes, he did."

"Your skills, please." She tapped on her tablet, her finger poised over the screen.

I listed all of them aloud.

When her finger eventually stopped moving over the screen, her dark gaze peered up at me in surprise. "That is impressive."

I shrugged and nibbled on my lower lip again.

Her gaze ran over my features. "I take it you want to be in the infantry?"

"No." I instantly shook my head. "I'd like to go

into your intelligence unit."

She stared. "But your skills are infantry related."

"I can hold my own in a fight. I agree. And, yes, I could be a major asset for the Corporate Army in the infantry." I shrugged again. "But I like puzzles. When I pass these tests, I plan to test for the intelligence unit."

Her lips twitched. "*When* you pass these tests?"

I hesitated, remembering what that guard had said. "Respectfully, of course, ma'am."

There. That sounded nice.

She smiled, but it wasn't pleasant. "Do you really believe playing with puzzles qualifies you for our most elite unit?"

"I think it matters if I pass their exam."

Shit. That was a little rude.

Eh... I was being myself.

Her smile reached her eyes now, though. "Ms. Carvene, you may go back to dinner." She tapped her screen. "You've passed your first test."

CHAPTER FIFTEEN

It was so early in the morning the sun hadn't peeked over the horizon, but the sky was turning a beautiful pink at the edge. Early rising didn't bother me. I was used to it living on military bases. But not everyone agreed with my living style.

The candidates near me were dragging their feet as we began our march down the walkway to the sidewalk. I'd finally showered, and I smelled decent. Everyone had been given uniforms consisting of black cargo pants, white t-shirts, and black boots. I wasn't allowed to wear my ball cap, so I simply kept it in my left back pocket and pulled my hair up into a ponytail.

My hair swung back and forth brushing my shoulders with each bounce of my step. The girl next to me glowered at my perkiness. I smiled with cheerful delight to annoy her further.

None of the candidates had done anything horrid to me so far, so I had managed a full night's sleep. The bed wasn't big, but it was soft. I had fallen asleep as soon as my head hit the pillow.

We turned right outside of the gate and walked as a group down the sidewalk. The five CA soldiers who had interviewed us, and who were clearly our instructors, were leading our little event. They hadn't said where we were going, only banged on our doors for breakfast when it was still completely dark outside.

A flash of silver caught my eye.

I narrowed my gaze on one of the small trees planted for decoration on the opposite sidewalk. There was a silver furry tail sticking out behind the trunk. I blinked in astonishment as my train companion stuck his head around the tree, his silver eyes watching the parade of candidates.

I pointed to where he was. "That fox is following me. I swear it."

The girl I had annoyed snorted. "You're crazy."

"You see it, right?"

"Yes."

"Well, it's following me."

She watched as the fox darted from behind one tree to the next, his silver eyes watching my movement. "Okay, that is a little weird."

"Exactly."

Then I remembered I wasn't supposed to make friends, and I shut my mouth. But I kept a wary eye on my silver stalker. I had no clue how he had found me amidst the masses in New City.

Two turns later, our group stopped.

In front of King Corporation.

I squinted at the building.

People were already entering, the sun now rising.

One of the male CA instructors took the lead from the front of our group as we all congregated on the sloping hills of grass. "Listen up. We're touring King Corporation today."

Cheers erupted from my peers.

No. No. No. No.

This couldn't be happening.

My chest constricted as my pulse raced. I did not want to go in there where *he* might be. That was the last confrontation I wanted right now in front of the instructors who would decide if I 'passed' their tests. I kept my gaze on the entrance of the building and shoved my hands into my pockets to hide their shaking.

Worst. Day. Ever.

The instructor patted the air to quiet the excited candidates. The clamor finally died down, and he continued, "All female recruits will be with our female lead, Major Anne Wilcox. For the males, we'll be calling off your names, and which of us will be giving you the tour. Everyone will all see the same things today but merely at different times. You will be free to eat lunch wherever you wish, but we want you back in this same spot by two o'clock. Do you understand?"

I muttered, "Yes, sir."

The rest yelled it.

"Female recruits, go with Major Wilcox."

The girls started moving through the crowd, myself included. I should have watched where I was walking.

"Shit," I grumbled as I stumbled into the guy's back in front of me. I quickly righted myself and pulled my hands out of my pockets, holding them up in the air when he glared. "I'm sorry. Little distracted."

He sneered. "Watch yourself, Carvene."

"Gotcha." I nodded quickly.

I paid attention this time as I maneuvered through the group, a few elbows jutting out and jarring my body just as I stepped by.

The foul play was starting.

Major Wilcox waited at the front of the building until all ten women lined up side-by-side. "Don't touch anything that you're not supposed to. Don't speak to anyone you're not supposed to. And do not wander off while we're in here. You follow me, not the other way around. There are cameras everywhere that will be watching your every move." Her dark eyes peered at each one of us in turn. "Do you have any questions?"

The girl next to me stood with her hands behind her back in full soldier stance. "Yes, ma'am. I have a question."

Major Wilcox waited, one of her eyebrows lifting.

"Will...um." The girl rocked back on her heels,

then steeled her courage. "Will we get to meet Mr. King today?"

Fuck, I hoped not.

I scratched at my forehead.

Dropped my hand when I realized I was fidgeting.

Major Wilcox stated, "He is in the office today, but he doesn't speak with recruits, only his top senior staff. He's an incredibly busy man, and his time is always taken with meetings. Any other questions?"

I nibbled on my bottom lip.

The acid in my stomach was rising.

I prayed I didn't see him.

No one else spoke up.

She turned and muttered under her breath, "That's always the only damn question." Her voice rose so everyone could hear her. "Let's go, ladies."

CHAPTER SIXTEEN

The buzzer beeped indicating my body scan was approved, and the guard at the door allowed me entry into the grand lobby of King Corporation. I kept my head down, covertly glancing at each person inside while we waited for everyone to be checked for hidden weapons. They weren't allowed in this building—a new one for me. Only Corporate Army soldiers were allowed weapons in here.

Major Wilcox had bypassed the scan, her swords in full view. She nodded at the guard, smiling at him. "See you later, George."

"Later, Anne."

They were chummy. Good for them.

I kept to the middle of our small group as we walked further into the opulent main entrance. The area was wide and open, the ceiling three stories tall. There were splashes of blue in the elegant ivory tiling. Plants and long blue cushioned benches were placed on the outer edges and the back wall near the elevators. An ivory, half-moon concierge desk sat in the center of the room for anyone with questions, the woman behind the desk dressed in black business attire.

The main floor was simple. And elegant.

Expensive.

It also allowed many, *many* people to stand and talk with one another. I couldn't even see everyone the farther we walked, our destination the elevators. A quiet murmuring started around us, though, and the whispers were excited. I didn't like the anticipation of the crowd's demeanor.

Major Wilcox turned to face us, stopping our progress, and practically rolled her eyes. "Apparently, we will have a Mr. King sighting." She tipped her head behind us. "I believe I heard he's walking through the door now."

Fuck no.

I quickly ducked out of our group, completely unnoticed with all the tall people standing around. With sweat beading my brow, I weaved as quickly as I could to the back of the room. There had been a restroom sign somewhere along the wall. My eyes darted, scanning as fast as I could.

There it was.

I ducked inside just as two women ran out the door in a hurry. They were certainly Mr. King fans from the way they straightened their skirts and finger-combed their hair in a rush. I shut the door quickly and glanced under the stalls looking for feet.

No one else was in here with me.

I opened the door a crack to peek outside.

The crowd parted, and he was there strolling through the lobby. No one overtly stared at him, all pretending they were still talking with their co-workers. Godric acted as if no one else was around except for the four men he was walking and laughing with. They all wore pristine suits, but those were certainly tailor made because those men were just as muscled as Godric was.

He and his friends were frightening.

And sexy. All of them a treat to the eye.

I ground my teeth together when Major Wilcox pulled the ladies from their ogling and took them to the elevators. The elevator chimed too soon, and they all disappeared inside. What floor they were going to, I hadn't a damn clue.

But I couldn't move since Godric's group had stopped in the middle of the lobby to discuss bullshit for all I knew.

My red brows furrowed as I watched.

Godric paused and sniffed the air.

He blinked ever so slowly and began looking at each person outside of his group. His tawny curls brushed his shoulders as his head turned to the side in his perusal, allowing me a great view of his profile. The bastard was just as striking to look at in the morning light.

One of his friends with white hair touched his arm and asked him a question, apparently noticing his distracted state.

Godric held up a quick finger, shushing him. He sniffed the air once more, and then his steps were measured when he started walking again, his black dress shoes silent on the tiling. Right in my damn direction.

I quickly shut the door. "Shit. Shit. Shit."

My wide eyes stared at the ivory door as I slowly backed away from it. He wouldn't go in the ladies' room. That didn't make any sense. I froze in the middle of the bathroom when the door banged open, caught by the predator.

Godric stopped in his tracks, his nostrils flared. Golden eyes pierced mine for a full half minute while he just stood in the entrance, his hand still holding the door open.

The man with the white hair cleared his throat from outside and peered around Godric's head toward me. "Is there an issue, God?"

"God?" I blinked then. My voice was full of derision. "I know you're an egomaniac, but you don't seriously let people call you that, do you?"

The furious man finally spoke, growling, "Get your ass over here right now, Poppy." Apparently, he didn't want to move further into the ladies bathroom.

"No, I'm good." I took a step back.

I was wrong.

Godric slammed the door behind him and charged right at me, the sleeves of his black suit jacket straining against his clenched muscles. He grabbed ahold of my right bicep and flat out started dragging my ass toward the door.

My boots skidded along the tiling as I pulled back, but it was no use. "Dammit, let go!"

Then he opened the door to the bathroom.

We were outside it with one more step.

His four friends had created a barricade so no one could watch the show occurring with their favorite man on earth. Four pairs of eyes stared down into my flushed face as I kept jerking my arm inside his hold. Then their brows furrowed as they inhaled deeply.

Pure shock radiated off them, their eyes widening.

The one with white hair stared at my neckline where my shirt was askew from Godric's brutal ways. He muttered in surprise, "Fuck. It's about time. And look at that bite."

"Shut the hell up, Finn." Godric turned his angry gaze down on mine, and his voice lowered. "Stop fighting me, or you are going to make a scene."

I glared but quickly quit struggling.

There was another group of recruits being scanned at the front entrance. I didn't want any of them taking notice.

Finn blinked, his eyes focusing. "What now, God?"

I snorted. I couldn't believe they called him that.

Godric groused, "I'm taking her up to my office."

"We have a meeting scheduled."

"It can wait."

He kept his grip firm on my bicep, herding me to the elevators. His friends managed to keep everyone from seeing me, their muscled bodies perfect as a blockade. Godric glared down at me while waiting for an elevator to arrive, no words spoken.

The elevator dinged. All six of us piled inside.

Godric and I were in the back.

The floor numbers on the screen above the doors continued to flash red as they went higher and higher.

His friend with the black hair glanced back and blatantly analyzed my body. "What's her name?"

"Fuck off, Rune," Godric growled.

Rune tipped his eyes up to his friend, a cunning grin gracing his handsome features. "So you are possessive of this little waif of a girl. Interesting." He smirked when Godric yanked me a step closer. "She's not your typical lover. You look like you'd break her."

I stiffened at the jibe.

The man with brown hair choked on a laugh, not even peering back. "Fuck, Rune. That's harsh." He paused. "But I'm betting he took soft care with her."

"Alaric, you can fuck off too." Godric cracked his neck.

"Actually, I did think he looked a little different this morning." The last of his friends decided to join in this discussion—if you could call it that. It was more like best friends teasing one another. The man with gray hair shrugged, staring up at the numbers still rising. "His cheeks were rosy and shit."

Godric sighed. "And fuck you too, Wolfe."

I tapped my right foot in irritation.

"Okay," I growled. "I have feelings, and I'm right here. Your comments were extremely rude and hurtful."

The men fairly vibrated in front of me with barely contained laughter. Alaric even snorted, his brown hair shaking with it. The other three weren't faring much better.

My temperature rose, and my hands shook. "Do you *know* who I am?"

Godric rubbed at his temples with his free hand.

Rune muttered, "Yes, you're his fuck buddy. Even if his cock could splinter your sweet little pussy in two." He shook his head in mock sympathy. "Really, sweetheart, you might have fangirled with my man here. But he's too much of a brute for you."

My nostrils flared. "I'm Poppy Carvene, asshole."

The elevator halted, just as it went completely silent inside. I grinned in malicious delight. "That's right. Carvene, you pricks. And believe me, there was no fangirling for your *man* here when I found out who he was. I'm pretty sure the feeling is mutual for him too. So shut your damn mouths."

The elevator doors opened on the top floor.

They stood frozen in place, not moving.

Blocking our way with their blank expressions.

Godric growled with hostility, "Get out!"

CHAPTER SEVENTEEN

Godric didn't release my arm when we stepped out of the elevator. His fury continued to rise with each step he took to a waiting area on our left behind a glass wall. The flare of his nostrils was impressive, along with the pink flush to his dark complexion. He yanked the glass door open and hauled me inside.

His friends, now carefully mute, followed us in and began taking seats in the room. They watched me with distrust in their eyes, not looking away. It was slightly intimidating with all that masculinity watching me like they were going to attack at any minute.

An assistant sat behind a desk identical to the one in the main lobby. He peered up from his work, a small look of surprise flashing in his eyes when he saw Godric pulling me along behind him.

"Sir, is there anything I can get you?"

"Just hold my calls, Reed. And cancel my seven o'clock meeting," Godric griped. He opened the lone door and shoved me inside the room. He followed me in and peered out the door, ordering, "No one disturbs me."

He slammed the door shut, and barked, "Lock."

Wonderful.

I was locked in a room with my father's enemy.

Godric turned to face me and unbuttoned his suit jacket. He leaned back against his door and crossed his arms over his impressive chest. His golden regard scanned my features, and then he stared hard into my eyes.

"I know we said we would contact each other again, but after what happened, I didn't expect you to come to me." His voice was restrained calm. "So what are you doing here, Poppy? Are you spying on me?"

I rubbed at my bicep. I'd have a definite bruise there. "Are you joking? I don't want to be here any more than you want me here."

The brows on his forehead rose. His beautiful voice enticed me to tell the truth. "So you're saying you were brought to my place of business against your will?"

I clicked my teeth together and grimaced. "No."

"Then what are you saying?"

He was excellent at interrogating, his patient hunting maddening. All that hostility he had tucked away to get the answers he wanted. No emotions now showed on his features, his eyes even clearer, only intelligence lurking in their golden depths.

I shook my arm out to make the blood flow in it again. "Did you really have to hold me that tight?"

"You were going to cause a massive scene downstairs. That wouldn't have been good for either of us. I did what I needed to get you here. My office is soundproof." He tipped his head. "Now quit deflecting. Why are you here?"

I sighed and turned to walk to his desk. His office was just as ridiculous as the crown on the roof. Expensive items were everywhere—on his bookshelves, his desk—the couches were leather and even his lighting fixtures were over the top lavish. I picked up a baseball on his desk and tossed it up and down as I peered back to him. "Why do you let them call you God?"

Godric didn't comment on my change of topic. He rolled effortlessly with it. "Rune stuck me with the nickname many years ago. There is no stopping it with those four. But I blame my parents for naming me Godric in the first place."

I put the baseball back down in its proper place. "It's a nice name. Don't be too mad at your parents."

He hummed, watching me evaluate his stuff.

Waiting for me to answer his question.

I picked up another item on his bookshelf and showed it to him. "What's this? It doesn't look like an ordinary knife."

"It's a letter opener. People once used them when they received paper mail to their homes. It would slice an envelope, what a letter was carried in, opening it much cleaner than tearing it with your fingers."

"Hmm." I put it back down and touched more of the items, all of them shined with care. "So you collect old things?"

"Of a sort."

I sighed and turned to him. Enough stalling. "I'm here because I'm a recruit for the Corporate Army. We're doing a tour here today. And I'm now going to be in trouble for 'wandering away' from the group."

He didn't blink. "The Corporate Army?"

"Yes."

Wrinkles on his forehead showed his confusion, no longer hiding his emotions with the answer given that he'd wanted. "General Carvene would never agree to that."

I nibbled on my bottom lip and glanced away.

In the resulting quiet, he started to chuckle. It was wicked and soft. "That's a bad girl, pet."

The endearment was back.

"Running from Mr. Moore, are you?"

I cleared my throat and pretended to examine another one of his collectibles, not looking at him.

He didn't quit. "But you did seem to like your fiancé's appearance. I believe you even blushed at one point."

"Don't call him that," I griped.

I turned with my mouth open, ready to argue the

injustice of arranged marriages. But I stopped in my tracks.

Godric peered down at me with his golden eyes, only an inch away from me. I hadn't heard him move. His heat pulled at me, and I stepped closer, removing the gap between us. Our bodies aligned just right. The lushest lips curved up at the edges in the sexiest smirk.

He asked, "What else were you going to say?"

I stared at his chest straining the buttons on his white dress shirt with each heavy inhale he took. "That corporations are the reason I had to run away. It's your law that makes women marry by the age of twenty-five."

"If it wasn't there, this world would vanish."

"Women should be able to marry whenever they want. And definitely not to someone their father picks for them."

"The planet needs more children. Adults are dying faster than babies are born, thanks to lawless activity outside of our cities. Do you want the world to end?"

"No." I closed my eyes. My shoulders slumped.

He purred softly, "Look at me, pet."

I shook my head and kept my eyes closed. "I know what you want. And we can't do that. It's a horrible idea."

He hummed in thought. "Are you afraid of your father?"

I snorted. "Never."

"Are you afraid of what he would think?"

"Of course."

He whispered on the deepest rumble, "Then we won't tell him."

The man was pure temptation.

"That's not all of it." I opened my eyes and lifted my head to peer into his wondrous golden gaze. "I don't trust you. And if word ever leaked... It wouldn't be good, big man."

He held my eyes with a steady and patient gaze,

even though heat simmered in those golden orbs. "Do you want to know something?"

"I'm not sure." I eyed him carefully.

He smirked. "I'm going to tell you anyway."

"I thought you would."

Godric dipped his head down close to my face, his warm breath fanning over my lips. "You're still going to fuck me again and again despite all your reservations."

My snort was soft. "Why is that?"

"Because you want to. You want the right to choose your fate and who you are with. And you will choose me because you can't seem to help yourself when you're around me." He leaned lower, pressing his mouth against mine, moving his lips against my lips while he spoke. "And I can't seem to help myself either, even though you're right. This is an extremely bad decision. And I still don't give a fuck."

CHAPTER EIGHTEEN

I moaned in need, my lower stomach heating deliciously. I pressed myself hard against him and ran my hands up his chest to grab hold of the lapels of his suit jacket. I wanted him to kiss me as much as I needed to breathe. His natural scent surrounded me, full of wild spice and cherries. I wanted to lick him all over.

I groaned, "Kiss me."

Godric pounced at my acceptance. His arms wrapped around me and lifted me off the floor. I wrapped my legs around his waist and held tight to his suit jacket as he pressed my back against his bookshelf.

He tilted his head and kissed my lips just how I wanted. Like I was his favorite dessert. His tongue touched mine and glided with sensual hunger, battling for dominance. He needn't have worried. I submitted to him in a heartbeat, my body quivering against his.

I rubbed myself on his hard muscles. "*Yes.*"

"Mmm." He moaned and slid his hands down to my ass, holding me close against his erection. "I want you, pet."

I groaned in frustration and leaned away. My head tipped back, and I stared at his ceiling. "I don't have time. Major Wilcox will kick me out if I don't get back to her group."

He sucked on the side of my neck with gentleness. "I can order her not to."

I grabbed ahold of his hair and pulled his face back to stare into his eyes. "Don't you dare. I want to make it in the CA on my own. I don't want another man interfering in my future."

His eyes narrowed. "You are rather stubborn."

"At times." I leaned forward and kissed his lips once more. "I really need to get going now. I'll have to find her in this huge ass place."

"That, I can help you with." He leaned heavily against me, smashing my body against the bookcase, as he placed his forehead on my shoulder. Then he mumbled in his own frustrated tone, "Order: Call Reed."

His bracelet buzzed.

"Yes, sir?" His assistant's voice was clear.

"Do a search to find where Major Wilcox is in the building right now."

His bracelet went quiet, then Reed stated, "Sixteenth floor. East wing. The CA section."

"What is she doing there?"

Another quiet moment. "Running a search for a Ms. Poppy Carvene in your building."

I stiffened in his arms.

Godric ordered, "Cut the electricity in there now."

"Done."

"Create a malfunction with their recording devices for today, all recordings deleted in their database. Send the originals to only me before deleting them out of your system."

"I will make a note to do that tonight, sir." He paused. "Is there anything else you need?"

"Nothing right now. Order: End call."

His bracelet buzzed once more.

I nibbled on my bottom lip. "You do realize he was talking to my ass?"

Godric squeezed said ass. "Then he's a very lucky man." He lifted his head and kissed my neck before easing me to my feet. He ran a hand through his tawny curls, his brows furrowed. "If you decide you want me to straighten out the situation with Major Wilcox, I will. Just let me know."

I patted his chest. "I can take care of it."

He bent and grabbed my ball cap that had fallen out of my back pocket at some point. He held it out to me, eyeing the old thing. "You should really get a new hat. That one is falling apart."

I quickly snatched it from his hand and put it into my back pocket. My eyes held his with a new simmering anger. "It was my mom's."

His nostrils flared as he stared down at me.

Everyone knew that my mother was dead, just like everyone knew General Carvene would never back down against Mr. Godric King. The corporations had stalled giving Port proper medical equipment when one single invoice had slipped through their hospital's accounting program and wasn't paid.

My mother had died because of that.

The invoice had only been twenty-two units.

Godric opened his mouth and then shut it.

I ground my teeth together. "There's nothing you can say to make her death okay."

"I know." He actually sounded regretful.

My voice turned sarcastic. "Though, it was awfully nice of you to fix that little glitch in your purchasing program after she died. I'm sure you save many lives now that your technology doesn't withhold medical equipment from those in need."

His eyes flashed on mine. "Don't."

We glowered at one another. Ice and fire.

Together we sizzled with our past.

I stepped around him and walked to the door on stiff legs. With my back to him and my hand on the doorknob, I stated, "Unlock the door, Godric."

"Unlock." He didn't hesitate.

I jerked the door open and walked out.

Each one of his friends sniffed the air heavily and

watched me as I walked by them before turning their attention back to Godric's office.

"Poppy, I do expect you to answer when I call." Godric's delicious voice was hard in demand, stopping me in my tracks.

I glanced at him over my shoulder, not commenting.

He raised one brow, and he leaned against the doorframe and crossed his arms. "Everything we talked about in there? We already knew."

I stared with perfect calmness. "I know."

"You'll answer then."

I nodded.

One side of his lips curved up.

"I do have one question before I have to grovel."

"Go ahead."

"How did you know I was in the bathroom?"

Humor lit his gaze. "I smelled you."

I blinked. "That's not funny. I don't stink."

He grinned. "No, you don't."

"Then how?"

"I already answered you."

"You're going to stick with that?" My voice was dry.

"I guess I am."

I sighed and walked out the glass door.

That man was in a league of his own.

It was time to pray Major Wilcox didn't boot me.

CHAPTER NINETEEN

"I know," I stated in a soft tone. "I am so sorry. But when Mr. King came in the building, I lost you guys in the crowd. One minute you were there, the next you weren't."

Major Wilcox glared down at me, her hands on her hips next to her swords. "And it took you this long to find us?"

"It's a big building," I explained.

She hadn't been on the sixteenth floor when I arrived there. The halls had been dark; only tiny emergency lighting lit the hallways. I had to search the place based on where I believed the instructors would take candidates on a tour. I was lucky to find them on my first shot—the history section where they were learning all about how Godric had first formed the corporations after the final war.

The major still glared.

I shoved my shoulders back. "I found you fast."

And I had. I was proud of myself.

Her tone turned dry. "You shouldn't have lost us in the first place, Ms. Carvene." Her dark eyes peered heavenward, and she sighed with resignation. "Mr. King can have that effect on people. You aren't the first person to have been star struck when seeing him for the first time. There was this one time two trains ran into one another when a guy crossed the street right between them, all to get Mr. King's autograph."

My lips trembled. "Seriously?"

She snorted. "There are more ridiculous stories."

I held up a quick finger. "For the record, I wasn't star struck. I just got shoved back really far in the crowd." I shrugged my right shoulder. "I didn't think it would be appropriate to start fighting King Corporation employees at that moment. Mr. King was nearby, after all."

Little lies. Little lies.

Back to the dry tone. "Wise choice." She tilted her head to where the other nine female candidates were waiting—far enough away not to overhear our conversation. "Get in line with the others, but don't even think about losing us again, Ms. Carvene. If you do, you're out."

"Yes, ma'am." I bowed my head to her and then hurried to stand next to the last girl in our line. I breathed a sigh of relief and ignored the nasty glances the others shot in my direction. Their tour was put on hold for a whole two minutes. *The nerve I had!*

I didn't roll my eyes. Barely.

Major Wilcox marched down the line and just kept walking, expecting us to scurry after her. "Listen up, recruits. We're heading to the technology center next, where the best scientists in this world work their magic to create a better living for us." She paused in her speech to peer back at us. And we did, indeed, hurry like ants after her. "I think this bears repeating... Don't wander off."

The girls flashed glares back in my direction.

I simply pretended they didn't exist.

* * *

A scientist droned on and on.

Mr. King this...

Mr. King that...

Oh! Did you know Mr. King...

This idiot was star struck.

I was embarrassed for him. I wanted to pat his back and tell him it was all right to have a little obsession, but perhaps he should look outside of New City for one. Or even the King Corporation. Many other individuals in the world had helped to reinstate our planet after it went to shit. It wasn't all Godric the Great.

Godric was only around thirty years old. The way this scientist spoke about him, it was as if Godric had ended the damn war one hundred and fifty years ago. He was just that special to have done all this before he was even born—or his parents were even born. Perhaps star struck didn't explain this silly scientist appropriately enough, as he continued rambling on with shining eyes of faith. I was thinking a white straightjacket might be needed if he didn't calm himself, and maybe Godric needed extra security to watch out for this loon.

I was distracted—thank goodness—when a man exited a door at the end of the hallway. There was no sign on the door indicating what the area was, but with the CA soldiers posted outside the door, I was betting it was a confidential post. The man towered in height and had a dark olive skin tone, with broad shoulders and muscles that bulged on his biceps beneath his short-sleeved black t-shirt. He wore dark jeans and had a smooth gait as he walked down the wide hallway in our direction. He wasn't dressed in a suit like almost all the employees I had seen so far—which wasn't a whole lot thanks to Godric dragging me off. He even wore black flip-flops on his tan feet.

His head of short, dark honey-colored hair was lowered as he stared down at his silver bracelet, typing on it. I couldn't guess his exact age, but he appeared no older than twenty or maybe thirty, his facial features plain but striking at the same time. He strolled past us without looking up, still typing on his bracelet.

Except he pivoted when he was three feet past us,

still staring at his watch, and ambled to stand directly behind our group. He leaned back with his shoulders against the wall, crossed one foot over the other, and stayed there while he worked on his bracelet.

The girl I had spoken to about the stalker fox glanced back at him with her eyebrows down, also having noticed the oddity. She eventually shook her head, dismissing him, and turned her attention back to the blathering, almost clinically insane, scientist.

I kept my attention on the guy, though, and watched him from the corner of my eye. He blended extremely well, enough that no one else took notice of him, but there was something about him that sent a shiver down my spine. And not in a good way.

He eventually stopped looking at his bracelet, crossed his arms over his chest, and peered up, as if he were listening to the scientist too—though his dark eyes began to journey over our group with extreme slowness. Far before his sharp gaze landed on me, I looked away and actually listened to the recited speech. I could blend too, and I didn't want his eyes on me.

After five more minutes, I peeked in his direction.

He had finished with his overall perusal and was now evaluating the two girls in the middle of our group. His eyes traveled over their short black hair, their breasts that strained their t-shirts, and down their long shapely legs. There wasn't heat in his eyes, his regard not sensual. It was an appraisal of their persons, their every detail categorized by his attention.

His head lowered once more when he uncrossed his arms and started playing a game on his bracelet, completely at ease. He even had a little smirk on his lips.

The scientist finally concluded his talk of Godric the Great. By this point, I wasn't the only one in our group who breathed a sigh of relief. My back was even killing me from standing still for so long. I stretched high and leaned back while a few of the other women shook out their legs and arms.

Major Wilcox announced, "Line up, recruits. Next on our list is a short video of how the new technology will shape our future."

"We can finally sit down," the girl next to me muttered. Same gal I had talked to before.

I snickered and nodded in agreement, keeping my voice low. "Maybe the video will also include something other than how wonderful Mr. King is."

She ducked her head and snorted. "That scientist was bad, wasn't he?"

"Fuck. Yes, he was." I kept stretching and waited for the end of the line as the candidates started filing behind Major Wilcox, her strides long as she marched down the hallway. I glanced at the girl. "What's your name?"

"Megan Marshall."

"Nice to meet you."

She eyed me with caution. "You too."

My lips twitched. "Not friends."

"Not friends. Not here," Megan agreed. She turned and took her place in line, and I followed her at the end.

The honey-haired man still had his head down, playing on his bracelet. Except his brows instantly furrowed when the two women he had been evaluating walked in front of him in our silent trek. When they finished ambling past him, he blinked slowly, his fingers never faltering on his game.

His head tilted, though, when I walked past him.

I kept walking but did glance back.

The man lifted his head, and his dark eyes landed directly on mine. He didn't look away when caught staring. No, those intelligent eyes of his ran over my features and body in a methodical progression, his brows rising high on his forehead in what appeared to be surprise.

I shivered as I turned the corner, out of sight.

He may be consistently overlooked because of his casual simplicity of appearance, knowing how to blend in well, but no one should ever dismiss him as anything but one scary ass man.

CHAPTER TWENTY

The green grass beneath me was supple and soft in the courtyard of King Corporation. I relaxed while I sat and crossed my legs, content with the sun shining down on me—with my sunglasses on. It was lunchtime, and we had an hour to eat, many King Corporation employees also eating their lunches out in the courtyard. It was a beautiful day with minimal cloud cover and just a touch of an indulgent breeze to keep you from becoming too warm. I lifted my cheap sandwich and took a bite while I brought up a puzzle game on my bracelet, switching it to hologram mode.

The screen appeared in front of me.

I nibbled on my sandwich with my left hand while I ran my fingers on the screen with my right. The game started, showing a picture of the world. I twirled my finger, and the earth spun onscreen.

When it stopped, a red dot appeared in the center of King Eastern Province. It zoomed in fast until I was staring at a ruined building in the heartland of the country. I ticked my finger around the building, as a minute timer started in the corner, and evaluated the structure at every angle, looking for clues. Then the world faded, the timer run down. It brought up a puzzle with multiple different answers on the vast pieces.

I quickly picked the pieces for how I believed the building was destroyed and watched as they formed together.

I was missing one piece to make a full square.

I took another bite and chewed slowly.

A shadow blocked the sun above me.

My brows rose as Godric the Great sat down next to me on the grass. His four friends were also with him, their hulking forms agile as they sat down at his side and in front of him. They had all brought their lunches, and five pairs of big hands started arranging their meals in front of where they sat. The five of them had been deadly silent for me not to hear them sneak up.

And the man, the great man, was an idiot.

I pulled my sunglasses up on top of my head and glared at his profile, hissing, "What are you doing?"

"I'm eating my lunch." Godric grinned. His features were captivating to the extreme with his tan skin magnificent under the sunlight. He stared down into my eyes and licked his red bottom lip.

My eyes ogled it in fascination.

Rune glanced up beneath his black hair and smirked. "You technically haven't started eating yet."

Godric snorted and popped a strawberry into his mouth. "There, you fuck. Now I'm eating."

My gaze darted to the employees sitting in the courtyard, a few taking notice of their revered boss outside, though there were more than a few also eyeing his gorgeous friends.

I jerked my attention back to him, whispering, "This was not part of the plan."

Golden humored eyes twinkled in the sunlight, but his lyrical voice was sensual. "And what was that plan again?"

I growled deep in my throat.

His lips curled into a smirk. He popped another strawberry into his mouth and chewed as he ran his gaze over my features. Then he stated with calm, "There is nothing wrong with sitting together out in the open for lunch. The four horsemen of the apocalypse are with me, and you *are* a recruit for the Corporate Army and a person of importance in your own right. I'm sure that news is already traveling the world of your decision to join my army, so any pictures seen wouldn't be damning."

My molars were getting a workout today as I ground them together for the millionth time. "Joining your army and being 'friends' are two different things."

His eyes were cunning as they peered down at me. "Would you rather people think you work for me or are an acquaintance?"

I stalled.

"Exactly." He uncrossed his legs and placed his feet flat on the ground, his knees crooked up in relaxation. He pulled his food between his strong legs, ate another strawberry, and glanced at my paused game. "That's a good one."

I sighed and took another bite of my sandwich as his friends started talking to one another—when they knew they weren't leaving. "You've played it before?"

"Yes." He flicked a finger at Wolfe. "He designed that specific game."

My eyes widened on his fine-looking gray-haired friend. "Did you really make this one?"

Wolfe grinned, and his features altered from too handsome to sexy as fuck. "Yes. I'm the head of Cooper Corporation. Along with multiple technology programs, we create the puzzle games."

I stared in fascination. "You're Mr. Cooper?"

He bopped his shoulders with bored poise. "Yes, I'm Wolfe Cooper."

Oh, my.

I'd secretly been a fan of his for a long time.

Corporate or not, the man was a genius.

I'd read that he designed games in his free time.

That was apparently the truth.

Alaric chuckled, his eyes roaming my face. "Careful there, God. I think she has a crush on Wolfe, not you."

My cheeks instantly flushed. "It's not like that."

Godric asked smoothly, "What is it like?"

I blinked, still in awe. "He's a brilliant man."

Wolfe rolled his eyes. He tucked his gray hair behind his ears and tipped his head back to let the sun bask on his skin. "I merely enjoy what I do."

"And it shows," I said kindly. "Your games got me through... Well, they helped me when times were rough. Thank you for creating them for everyone to escape in."

He peeked at me from the corner of his eye. "You're welcome." Then he closed his eyes and let the sun shine on his face.

He wasn't a man of many words.

Godric grunted, jealous heat in his narrowed gaze. The muscles in his jaw clenched. He hissed in absolute possession, "She's mine, Wolfe."

Chapter Twenty-One

My mouth bobbed in surprise.

"I know." Wolfe chuckled, still sunbathing, not opening his eyes. "She doesn't look at anyone else the way she looks at you—not even when she calls someone brilliant. That wasn't intimate interest there, buddy."

Finally, I snapped out of my stupor.

I sniffed and peered down my nose at the group as a whole. "You are all ridiculous." My lips twitched. It was difficult keeping a straight face near them.

Finn grinned. "She's already got us pegged."

Godric scooched an inch closer to me.

I scrutinized his profile, my tone amused. "Don't worry there, big man. I heard all about your greatness today with every stop on the tour." I munched on another bite of my sandwich, thoughtful. "There's actually a scientist that you may want to screen better. He's a bit fanatical about you. Like, in a freaky ass way."

Alaric snickered. "I bet she's talking about Johnson."

I pointed at him with the remaining bite of my sandwich. "Yes. That was his last name."

Godric's shoulders eased, the tension flowing out of him. "There's already a restraining order against him. He's not allowed within twenty feet of me."

I knew it! Crazy science guy for the win.

"And you still allow him to work here?" I popped the last bit of my meal into my mouth, chewing and watching his eyes.

The pure arrogance that he was untouchable lived in their depths. "He's a mastermind, even if a little cracked when he doesn't take his meds. I want him on my team. I don't take intelligence for granted, no matter where it comes from."

I kept my eyes on his.

His on mine.

That was why he was so powerful, a little insight into the man. He knew how to use his resources to the best advantage—on his own terms. No one who disregarded skilled talent and outside thinking would ever be in power in the world we lived in.

I hummed quietly and smiled a little.

A clever man in the bedroom wasn't bad.

I was content with my choice to continue with him.

The game flashed a reminder to play again.

I turned my attention from him as I enjoyed the tiny smirk he graced me with, and then touched my fingers to the screen. Once again, I evaluated the choices of destruction.

I picked one. It was the right piece.

The earth spun on the screen.

I started over with a new destination.

Godric leaned against my shoulder and stared at the screen, eating a carrot now. One of his long fingers started to touch my screen, and I slapped it away. His chuckle was quiet as he watched me win again and again without his help, even once when I had guessed wrong.

"Is that sandwich all you had for lunch?" he asked in a quiet tone, his gaze still on my screen.

I tapped a destruction piece. "Yes."

"Why? You have an interesting evening planned." He finished his second carrot, the crunch not unpleasant to my ears while he chewed with his mouth shut. He swallowed it down a few seconds later. "You need your strength."

I sighed and evaded his question. "You looked at the CA schedule for the recruits?"

"I was bored." He shrugged, his shoulder rubbing against mine.

"I can only imagine," I muttered with sarcasm. But I lifted my left arm over his leg closest to me and stole one his carrots off the ground. I bit into it with relish, still ravenous. "Thanks."

His chest shook with silent laughter. "You're welcome."

I finished off the carrot and then leaned, peering down between his legs. My eyes widened in pure, astonished delight. "Is that peach cobbler?" Peaches were a rarity, a special and expensive treat you indulged in once every ten years—if you could afford them then.

His nose was close to my left temple with the way I was positioned. He whispered, "Take it."

I hesitated.

"You only have a chicken sandwich left then." I cleared my throat, and then mumbled as quietly as I could, "And I can't pay you back for that cobbler. I'm here with my own money, not my father's."

Heat burned on my cheeks as I blushed. Uncomfortable embarrassment thrummed inside my chest. But I really wanted that cobbler. I hoped he wouldn't say no. I was so broke now that I wouldn't be able to afford any meals outside of the Military House—it was free there.

Godric dipped his head forward, the tip of his nose now touching the tender skin of my temple. His voice was a mere breath. "Take it, pet. I want to watch that little pink tongue of yours lick every crumb off your delicious lips."

I peeked at his friends, but they were still deep in their own conversation. They hadn't heard what he said.

I seized the peach cobbler and the utensil next to it. Then I leaned back into my proper place. His shoulder still rested against mine, but we were no longer too close.

Around a mouthful of sinful indulgence, I mumbled, "Thank you."

His lips twitch. "You're welcome.

Golden eyes stared at my mouth.

Each time I licked my lips free of crumbs, his eyes flared in desire. He was enjoying watching me as much as I was enjoying eating. It was an excellent bargain.

Dark honey hair caught my attention as I licked the fork clean, the entire cobbler gone in less than a minute. The scary ass guy, who could pass for an academy student, was eating a piece of pizza by himself under a tree at a table.

I tilted my head in the man's direction. "Who is that guy?"

Godric's eyes flicked from my mouth to where I had indicated. He scanned the area with his intense gaze, many employees roaming the courtyard there.

"Which man?"

"The one by himself and eating pizza."

Godric found the target, and his brows rose when he peered back at me. "Most people don't notice he's around." His head tilted in interest. "Why are you curious about him?"

I didn't want him to know that the man scared me. I didn't want him knowing I found anything frightening. So I shrugged a bored shoulder, and answered, "He was hanging around when the crazy scientist was giving his speech about how amazing you are."

His lips twitched in humor, though his eyes carefully scanned my features. He didn't completely believe me. "His name is Theron. He works for me occasionally on special projects."

"Special projects?"

He nodded. That was all.

I knew a brushoff when I saw it.

Godric groaned under his breath, his features pained as he looked skyward. "Actually, I need to speak with him."

"Theron?" Finn groused. "Wait until we're gone."

Rune grunted in agreement, finishing his water.

Alaric rubbed his forehead. "I'm really not in the mood to deal with him today, either."

Wolfe snorted and glared. "Same."

My red brows rose on my forehead.

Their reactions were...interesting.

Finn growled and quickly looked away. He stared at the ground hard, picked at the grass near his crossed legs, and whispered swiftly, "Too late. He's headed this way."

I blinked in shock at his obvious anxiety.

All four of Godric's friends, and if I wasn't mistaken, all the powerful men in the corporations, gazed anywhere but at the man walking toward us in flip-flops.

I tensed and set my plate and my fork down.

Theron stopped in front of our group.

He was playing a game on his bracelet again, his head down without a care. His voice was quiet with an accent that sounded like sand blowing in a light breeze.

Theron stated directly in greeting, "Mr. King."

His gaze lifted. He didn't look at Godric.

Those dark eyes were honed directly on me.

I still couldn't figure out how old he was.

His attire was so innocent and casual.

His honey-colored hair gleamed under the sun.

And he definitely still scared the shit out of me.

Godric sighed. "Theron, this is Poppy."

The man didn't say anything, only started another one of his slow perusals of my person. When his regard rose back up my body and landed on my eyes, he smiled.

And it transformed his face into a masterpiece of beauty.

I blinked.

He. Was. Scary. As. Fuck.

Theron tipped his head to me. "It's an absolute pleasure to meet you, Poppy."

I nodded my head in a jerky motion.

I couldn't speak for the fear tightening my throat.

He stared. "A quiet one, huh?"

Godric chuckled. "Not exactly." He leaned closer to me, his shoulder bunched with protective muscle and warmth. "I actually need a favor."

Theron finally turned those eyes on Godric.

He complained, "I'm supposed to be on vacation."

"Yes. So you've said before. A hundred times. And yet you keep popping up at the most annoying times." Godric glared with an old argument that I knew nothing of, but I did know it was one by his irked expression. He paused and tapped his right foot. "So, are you willing?"

Theron peered back down to his bracelet. His tan fingers worked on the game with concentrated speed. "What is it?"

Godric sucked in a sharp breath, and then grumbled, "I'll be away for a few days with no contact. I need you to run this place while I'm gone."

I jerked my head in his direction.

What?

Who the fuck was this guy?

Theron's fingers kept tapping, his attention still on his freaking game. "Trouble?"

"No, nothing like that. It's personal."

Dark eyes did peek up then, even if his head was still lowered. A too-pleased smile lifted his lips.

Godric rumbled in exasperation, "Will you?"

"You'll owe me."

Godric's nostrils flared as he exhaled heavily through his nose. "The usual?"

"Yes. In a week." He tapped his bracelet, shutting off his game, and looked at the four silent men sitting before him. "That goes for the four of you too, since he's not asking you for this favor."

Four pairs of furious eyes shot to Godric and glared daggers. But they nodded their heads once in agreement.

Theron smirked as he strolled away, his flip-flops silent in the oddest way as he moved. "See you in a week, gentlemen."

We all watched him until he slipped inside the King Corporation, whistling the entire time as he strolled along, no one else even glancing his way.

"I hate you," Rune hissed.

Godric growled, "It's just dinner. Get over it."

My jaw went slack, and my eyes darted between all of them. "You five have to be the weirdest group I've ever met. That's saying a lot too because I've met some really freaky people all over the world." I flicked a finger where Theron had disappeared. "And I don't even know what the hell to think of him."

Other than he was a scary sonofabitch.

Godric huffed. "Just stay away from Theron."

"I planned on it." My head turned toward the sidewalk where Major Wilcox was now standing and checking her bracelet. I glanced at my own and quickly shut my game down. "I've got to go. Lunch is over."

Godric's golden eyes speared mine. "Take my sandwich with you. I'm not going to eat it."

I stared. "The test is going to be long, isn't it?"

He shrugged with nonchalance.

That was answer enough for me.

I leaned over his leg and grabbed the chicken sandwich. My thigh muscles ached as I stood up from sitting crossed legged for so long. "Thanks for the food."

"It was my pleasure."

I started walking, but I couldn't look away from his powerful regard. His eyes were gorgeous with the sun sparkling on the golden hue. My brows rose when his gaze widened, his mouth opening in a hurry, and his right hand shooting up in the air for me to stop.

Smack.

"Motherfucker!" I shouted and held the right side of my head. My eyes turned to glare at the tree I had run right into. I kicked the trunk, growling, "Fuck you and your scratchy bark too."

I kept rubbing my head as I marched.

Masculine roars of laughter erupted behind me.

I chose to ignore it—as I was doing a lot today.

The line was already forming with the other nine girls, so I quickened my pace and ate the sandwich as fast as I could. I chewed with such a large mouthful my cheeks were puffed out as I fumbled with my sunglasses. I finally got them over my eyes and stopped at the back of the line.

Major Wilcox strolled in a bored manner until she halted directly next to me. Her head tilted, and she asked, "Have a good lunch?"

Her fingers wiggled down by her sides.

I quickly took another bite, knowing what she was going to do. My cheeks were round once again, and my voice was muffled from the chicken. "Yes, ma'am."

"Good for you. It's over." The major moved fast as she yanked the remaining half sandwich out of my hands and chucked it into a wastebasket nearby. She bent and placed her face in front of mine, and whispered quietly, "I don't give a fuck who you sit with at lunch. When an order is given on my watch, you follow it. Do you understand me, recruit?"

Of course, she had noticed. Everyone had.

I swallowed the chicken down. "Yes, ma'am."

It was excellent.

I licked my lips for any lingering juices.

She glared at my pleased expression. "Do you find this funny, Ms. Carvene?"

"No, ma'am."

"Then why are you smiling?"

"Because my food was wonderful."

"Was it?" Major Wilcox mocked.

Then she jabbed me in the stomach.

I belched right in her face.

Megan choked next to me and quickly looked away.

I hastily covered my mouth with my hand, the most horrified expression on my face.

"I am so sorry, ma'am."

She blinked as she straightened. "Peach cobbler?"

I didn't remove my hand from my mouth as my other one rubbed my belly where she had poked.

"Yes, ma'am."

Her grin was wicked.

Shit.

"Okay, recruits." She peered down the line of candidates. "Ms. Carvene here had peach cobbler today. And not only did she enjoy it, but she also didn't share it with anyone. So I'm going to teach you all a little something about sharing."

Major Wilcox stared straight down at me, even as she talked to the entire group. "We're all going to share the love of running. Right now. Seven miles. If you stop, you're gone."

She yanked my sunglasses from my face and tossed them into the wastebasket too. "Those aren't regulation, Ms. Carvene." Then she snapped her fingers at the group, her voice rising to a shout. "What are you waiting for, recruits? Share! Share!"

The front of the line started jogging.

Major Wilcox winked at me. "Isn't this fun?"

"Yes, ma'am," I answered through clenched teeth.

She started running as the middle began.

Megan glanced back over her shoulder. Glared.

"Fuck," I groaned.

I peeked out of the corner of my eye.

Godric and gang were watching.

They'd had an excellent view too.

The only plus side?

They weren't laughing this time.

CHAPTER TWENTY-TWO

Damn. I should have been running more in Port.

I groaned as I rolled out of bed at the dinner bell. My hair was still wet from my shower, and I wore my pajamas—a simple pair of loose cotton pants and a tank top. I grabbed Godric's sweater as an afterthought and shoved it on over my head since the top of my shoulder still looked gruesome from his bite. Little scabs had formed, but it would scar. His teeth had sunk in too deep not to.

My slippers whispered on the hardwood floor, my feet dragging as I walked. The girls next to me weren't any better. We had lost two women, now down to eight female recruits, when the major had decided the last three miles were to be a sprint to the finish line. The two at the back had fallen and not gotten up, just lying on the concrete sidewalk and crying.

The men still looked in prime form around us.

They hadn't done anything extra after the tour.

I didn't even want to think about the test tonight.

Godric had acted as if it would be brutal.

And I was exhausted.

That wasn't a great combination.

I rubbed the back of my neck under my damp hair and ambled into the dining hall with the rest of the herd. When we were all inside, the doors locked behind us. I glanced around in confusion when there were no tables inside the room, much less food that I needed.

Whispers started around me, and a few men pointed to the far end of the room. My brows furrowed. I used my small size to squeeze between candidates, turning my shoulders, and brushing against their sides until I edged through the crowd to see what they were staring at.

Major Wilcox and her four counterparts were ignoring all of us as they spoke together near the far wall. But they weren't alone. Godric and Finn were both with them. All seven wore black martial arts pants. The male chests were bare while Major Wilcox wore a black tank top. They had no shoes on either.

There were weapons along the wall behind them.

Many different forms of weaponry. All deadly.

I tugged on the bottom of my sweater and attempted to keep my features blank, the skin on my cheeks tight with strain at seeing Godric here. If he was interfering with my chance to be part of the Corporate Army, I would have his damn balls. And if he was here to help me...

He would need help after I was done with him.

The kind of help that requires men to carry his casket.

Godric didn't look in our direction as he grinned at something one of the instructors had said, easily carrying on his conversation while a roomful of people waited.

Finn glanced at us and scratched at his chin, his eyes carrying over all the recruits he could see, evaluating them with experienced eyes. When his attention stopped on me, it was no different from all of the others he had assessed. Then he was on to the next individual.

He leaned in and said something to their group.

Every person laughed.

Yes, we were green.

I was in my damn pajamas, appearing for all the world like I was ready for a sleepover with a friend. Not at all like I needed to with a roomful of weapons. I was happy I had remembered to slide a hair tie over my wrist after showering.

The instructor in the middle eventually stepped forward when all of the candidates shut up about Godric being here. And Finn too. They had been arguing about who had the most impressive physique for fighting. No one had agreed on that one while I kept my mouth shut.

In my opinion, it was obviously Godric.

But they were both built like beasts.

The instructor stated loudly. "It's test time."

No shit.

"At least half of you will be leaving tonight."

That was nice of him to say.

"We will be calling names randomly. When your name is called, you can choose one weapon. Pick wisely because you will fight with it."

Hmm. That wasn't so bad.

"There will be no fatal blows."

Even better.

"The first person to draw blood wins."

Not so good.

"And the loser is out of the program."

That would definitely be bad.

There still had to be a catch. One on one was easy.

"Any questions?"

The man next to me raised his hand. "Will Mr. King and Mr. Baker be staying the entire time?"

I dropped my forehead into my right hand and rubbed at my temples. I could not believe the first question asked was that.

Baker. Baker, Baker, Baker...

It came to me quickly.

Baker Corporation. They were the largest weapons corporation, building and supplying the world's needs in the finest and deadliest weapons. I had thought Finn was the quietest and most reserved of Godric's friends. Perhaps he had a dark side he hid from the world running a dangerous business like that.

The instructor snorted. "Yes, they will."

I sighed and raised my hand before any other idiots could raise theirs. I asked in a bored tone, "Who will we be fighting?"

The instructor grinned. "Us."

I kept my hand in the air. "How many?"

"Our two against your one."

My hand loved high places. "How will you pick?"

"Randomly."

I wiggled my fingers still up there. "Do we need to bleed both people or just one?"

He snickered, amused with my persistence. "Both."

I finally lowered my hand.

Then I raised it fast with a thought. "Will we get dinner afterward?"

Finn's shoulders shook ever so slightly.

The amusement fled from the instructor's face. "Are you so sure you'll win?"

"Yes." I kept my hand up. "You didn't answer my question."

He sighed. "Dinner will be served afterward for those still here." His eyes scanned left to right on our group, skipping over me. "Does anyone else have any questions?"

My freaking hand was still in the air.

I lowered it and scowled.

When no one said anything, he nodded. "Good. Now please move to the outer edges of the wall and take a seat to wait your turn." Then he pivoted and chatted with their group once again, ignoring us all.

Megan tilted toward me, and questioned, "What else were you going to ask?"

I snorted. "The obvious. I wanted to know what was for dinner. I'm starving after that horrid run today."

CHAPTER TWENTY-THREE

My ass was numb by the time my name was called.

The time had afforded me what I needed, though.

I knew how they fought and which ones I didn't want to fight against. The two main people being Godric and Finn. Every time they had randomly been picked, the recruit was sent home. And they were holding back in each fight, the evidence clear in the tight coil of their muscles with each blow or pivot.

The view had been spectacular, though.

Both fought as if it were a fluid dance.

And Godric was hot as hell to look at too.

I stood and walked to the wall to pick my weapon.

This was the tricky part. None of the instructors or Godric or Finn had fought with the same weapon more than twice. They waited for the candidate to pick, and then they chose their own weapon.

I nibbled on my bottom lip.

The short sword seemed the easiest choice.

The whip the worst.

But I decided on the smallest blade available.

A pocketknife. No one had picked that yet.

I lifted it from the floor where it sat like a pebble amidst boulders. I opened it, and the silver gleamed— nice and sharp. I turned to Major Wilcox and held it up. "I choose the pocketknife."

All of my would-be opponents were much larger than I was, with longer arms and legs. They could easily reach me with a sword before I could reach them. That meant I would have to get in close and take away their main strength over me.

Major Wilcox stared. "You're sure?"

"Yes."

I strolled to the middle of the room and waited, the recruits still inside sitting against the walls, leaving plenty of room to fight in the middle. Now they just needed to pick who I was fighting against. I stretched my back while I watched them talk amongst themselves.

Major Wilcox wasn't pleased with the outcome.

Her brow furrowed and her cheeks flushed.

I saw why soon enough.

It was Finn. And herself.

She obviously thought Finn would let me win.

And he had better not.

If I lost, I wanted it to be an honest fight.

I watched the weapons they chose.

The major picked a short sword.

Finn decided on a smaller blade.

Her choice wasn't smart. His was.

I now knew where the real battle would be. It looked like I was getting that honest fight from him. I sat the pocketknife down and walked to the side of the room, removing Godric's baggy sweater and my slippers. Both would hinder my movements.

I yanked my hair up into a ponytail as I walked back to the center of the room. They were just arriving there. I jumped in place a few times before bending to pick up the pocketknife.

I closed it, the blade hidden from view.

Major Wilcox yanked her eyes from the savage bite on my shoulder to stare at the weapon I held. "What are you doing?"

"I'm going to take you down first. I don't need the blade for that." An evil grin lifted the corners of my lips as I let her see just how pissed I was for her actions today. "That sandwich was really good that you threw away and wasted."

The major shook her head in exasperation, not affected by my anger. "Just get ready, Ms. Carvene. It's time to begin."

I stood in place with my hands down at my sides.

The major stood on my right, and Finn took a position on my left. I didn't move, relaxed in my normal stance. They both judged my posture with a cynical eye.

The major growled, "I said get ready, recruit."

"I am. Start the damn fight already."

From the sideline, a male instructor barked, "Begin."

They charged at the same time.

I waited in place until they were closer.

Then I raced right at the major.

She pivoted and brought her sword down.

But I was already in her face, too close. I slammed the end of the closed pocketknife right against her nose. Blood instantly splattered with a sickening crack of bone. Still in motion, I flipped the blade out as I slid behind her right when Finn arrived, his blade flashing.

It was actually very simple. And I don't think he did it on purpose either. He hadn't expected me to use the major as a shield. Nor did he expect me to shove my foot against her back to send her colliding against him.

I stood still as he grunted and caught her.

And his arms were right there in front of me, stretching around the waist of the major. I merely flicked my wrist toward his left forearm, my blade connecting while I stood at ease. Blood slashed his skin in a red line.

Finn froze instantly with her still in his arms, his eyes wide in complete shock. The shock that was utterly real as he stared at me over her shoulder, not moving an inch.

The room was silent, no one speaking.

That was the fastest fight of the night.

I cleared my throat and walked back to the side of the room where the weapons rested. I sat the pocketknife on the table where it would be cleaned before put back to use again.

Godric was resting his shoulders back against the wall with his arms crossed over his massive, bare chest. The man was completely peaceful where he stood. He stared at me, his eyes quiet with no form of emotion showing on his face. Like I was no one to him.

He was the perfect visiting instructor.

My shoulders relaxed. I mentally cheered.

He wasn't here to influence in any way.

I spun to the instructor who had ignored me earlier, and I asked into the hushed room, "So what's for dinner?"

CHAPTER TWENTY-FOUR

My heart hammered in my chest as I jolted awake in the middle of the night. I instantly raced to the door and turned on my light, screams of dismay echoing in the hallways. I threw open my door to see multiple CA soldiers hauling candidates down the hall with their hands in cuffs behind their backs.

I stopped in my tracks, and my eyes widened.

What in the hell?

"I swear he signed the form," one male recruit yelled, struggling against the soldier pushing him down the hallway. His restrained arms thrashed back and forth. "This must be a mistake. I swear he did!"

"No!" Another male sobbed, pleading with the soldier behind him. Tears tracked down his flushed face; his shirt strained against his chest with his hands cuffed behind his back. "Please don't take me. He signed. He did. I promise."

My gaping mouth shut ever so slowly.

The instructors had indeed verified the signatures on the forms. And this was the fallout of those who had forged their male legal guardian's name. They were being hauled off to jail, their pleas ringing in my ears.

I stiffened as a CA soldier passed in front of me.

He kicked in the door right next to mine.

I held perfectly still as more soldiers filled the long hallway. Time was irrelevant when you were on the cusp of being caught. More rooms were entered, more candidates hauled away.

One of them was Megan.

When it eventually turned deathly quiet, and all of the soldiers were gone, I exhaled, and my body began to shake.

I repeatedly blinked at the candidate across the hall standing in his doorway just as I was. Whereas I was scared for my youth spent in a cell, he was starting to grin in glee for more competition gone.

There were now only four females left, myself included. Three females had been sent home from the fight test. And one had just been sent to jail. I was getting closer to my goal. But I was still vibrating in terror from that scene.

My father had saved my ass.

The five instructors, along with Godric and Finn, walked down the silent hallway. They wore black cargo pants, white t-shirts, and black boots—standard issue recruit attire. Except for that white splint on the major's nose. That one was all my doing, her nose broken in the fight. A few of the instructors had bandages on their faces or arms, just as Finn had a single bandage on his forearm. That one had been my fault too.

Godric didn't sport any bandages.

The same male instructor who had explained the rules of the fight test glanced up and down the hallway. His voice was loud as he ordered, "The criminals have been cleared out. I want all of you dressed and downstairs in five minutes. It's time for another test."

* * *

No one was tired even though it was two o'clock in the morning. All the recruits were wide-awake after that raid. No one spoke to anyone. Candidates were dropping off left and right, leaving no room for friendly behavior.

The male instructor's gaze ran over us from the stairs where the seven of them stood above us. He stated, "This trial will take place below Military House. We have a special training room set up just for this test. This one is our favorite. It will test your strength and your intelligence. You will sit down right where you are until we call your name to begin."

He didn't ask if there were any questions.

We didn't know enough yet to have any.

The instructor barked, "Sit, recruits!"

The shuffle of boots on tiling vibrated through the air as the remaining candidates sat.

I quickly followed suit, sitting and crossing my legs.

He nodded in satisfaction and walked down the stairs, the other instructors following behind him silently. He gazed down at his bracelet and tapped on it. The room was quiet as we waited for the first names picked from his random generator.

The instructor tapped his bracelet once more, and then he peered up. He announced, "Victor Hammond and Poppy Carvene."

At least my ass wouldn't be numb this time.

I stood to my feet and peered at the male who came to attention. I shuttered my gaze in a second. I had watched him today when he fought. Victor was excellent with his footwork, and his skills with a knife were intimidating.

"Follow us," the instructor ordered.

Victor and I followed the seven of them down a set of stairs off the main room. We didn't speak as we moved at a quick pace to keep up with the instructors. His legs were longer than mine were so I had to take two steps to his one, and I grunted in pain when I slammed my hand on a corner of a wall when we turned at the bottom.

Godric glanced over his shoulder as we continued trailing behind them. "Are you two behaving?"

"She's fine," Victor answered. "She just walked into a wall."

"I did not walk into a wall," I hissed in his direction. "It was my hand that hit it."

He shrugged. "Same thing."

I sighed and rubbed the top of my right hand.

They stopped and stepped into a room on our left.

Godric held the door open for everyone.

I was the last to enter.

When I passed him, the backs of his fingers grazed my side in an intimate touch. The only sign that he even knew me personally. He shut and locked the door behind us.

I stopped in my tracks and stared.

The room was huge, the ceiling tall.

And it had to be for what stood in the middle of it.

A raised glass enclosure in the shape of a rectangle. There were two enormous silver ventilation units attached to the top of it and two glass doors on either end. A round bullseye bag was inside sitting on an easel on the far side, and a lone knife was on the ground on the other.

The instructor stated, "Follow me, recruits."

The six other instructors took their seats on folding chairs next to the glass 'arena.'

I was intrigued despite myself.

He'd said it would test our intelligence.

It was a puzzle to me, my attention sharpening.

I hurried after him and climbed the six stairs quickly to where he was waiting for us on a small platform. I watched as he typed 1919 on the lock. Then we stalked with him inside the glass room, the floor made of only small metal grates.

He turned to face us. "I will only say this once. Don't touch anything in here before you begin. You will have one minute to choose your weapon." He pointed to a table outside the glass room where multiple weapons lay, and a bored soldier sat next to the table combing his hair. "Then you need to be back in here. You will fight each other to disable—your opponent must be unconscious. Try not to kill each other. Then you are required to use that knife on the floor to hit the bullseye dead center. Last, you will leave through the far door. Whoever is unconscious at the end is sent home."

He turned on his heel and walked to the door we had come in through. "Your time starts now."

CHAPTER TWENTY-FIVE

Victor raced from the glass room to the table of weapons.

I nibbled on my bottom lip as I studied the chamber I was in. The ventilation units on the glass roof were interesting as were the scratched up grates on the floor—since it was a raised room. I glanced at my opponent. His back was to me as he studied each weapon, and I hurried to the wall and sniffed at it. My eyes narrowed at the sour smell. The room had been used before, obviously, and I knew one more reason for the vents now.

I ran to the knife and peered at it, bending, and staring. There was a tiny piece of black metal beneath it. It was a trap for the unaware if you picked up the knife.

I hurried to the other side of the room and examined the bullseye, and, yet again, there were small black metal pieces beneath each leg of the easel.

My last stop was the door. I smirked. Easy.

Then I sprinted just outside the other door, squeezing past Victor as he walked in with a bat. That simple piece of wood was frightening in his hands. I stumbled down the steps in my haste and landed on my hands and my knees right in front of all the instructors sitting in their chairs.

"Dammit," I grumbled, not looking at them. I had been distracted by the freaking bat. The floor was freezing underneath my palms, and I shoved myself up to my feet.

I shook my hands out while I ran to the table and bounced from one foot to the other in front of it to loosen my muscles. My opponent stretched his inside the glass room. I chanted, "Little one, little one, little one."

There it was.

I grabbed the soldier's comb sitting on the table.

He didn't argue, so I knew I was right.

The instructor stared at his bracelet. "Five, Four..."

I sprinted across the floor.

"Three, Two..."

I clambered up the stairs.

"One..."

I jumped into the room just as the door automatically shut on its own behind me. I grinned in pure delight. "Whew. Made it!"

This was awesome fun.

Victor snorted. "Where's your weapon?"

I lifted the comb from my pocket. "Right here."

Then I stuffed it back down into my pocket.

He moved in a circle around me, his movements smooth and calm, and he chuckled. "That's not a weapon."

"You're right. It's a tool." Then I struck forward and grabbed him by his balls, even as he raised the bat to defend himself, squeezing and twisting as hard as I could. "My hands are my weapon."

He roared in pain and struck down with his bat.

I tilted my shoulders and stepped to the side.

The bat missed, and the tip banged on the metal grating as he doubled over in agony with his head hanging down.

I grabbed hold of his hair and yanked his face up, arched my back, and brought my elbow down in a cutting blow to the side of his head directly against his temple.

He fell like dead weight to the floor.

I tilted my head and picked up the bat, and nudged him with it. My opponent didn't move. He was definitely unconscious, hopefully without brain damage from my attack.

I dropped the bat next to his prone body.

Then I simply strolled to the knife.

It was time to hold my breath.

I sucked in a large lungful of air, keeping it trapped inside my lungs.

I bent down and picked up the knife.

An instant hiss escaped from the floor.

I turned quickly and positioned myself square with the bullseye. The exit was closest to this side of the room, so staying over here was ideal with the next booby trap coming.

I took aim and hurled the knife hard.

It hit dead center, embedding deep into the material.

Another hiss ejected from the floor.

I only saw a moment of yellow gas slithering up through the grates before I shut my eyes. My arms instantly shot out wide while I walked backward until my back hit the glass. I rolled on the wall to my left, not breathing and not seeing. Then I used my hands to crawl along the glass wall to guide me until I hit the exit.

My lungs started to burn, so I quickly pulled out the comb from my pocket. I felt along the comb until I found the smallest tooth. It snapped as I broke it off with a quick and efficient jerk of my wrists.

I dropped the rest of the useless comb on the ground and quickly ran my fingers along the lock. The numbers you didn't exactly type in, even though they were visually in the right place. You had to use the tip of a pen—or the teeth from a comb—for it to register your code. I kept my left hand on the device, using it as my eyes, and my right hand to punch in the numbers 1919.

Nothing happened.

I shook my head and tried again.

The vents above didn't turn on to suck the gasses out.

The door didn't open.

Exit... Exit... Exit...

An exit was the opposite of an entrance.

I started making the oddest noises, high and whining, as I fought not to breathe. It would happen, but I wouldn't go down without fighting my lungs for control.

I punched in the numbers the opposite way.

9191

The latch clicked. The vents whirled in power.

I jerked the door open and stumbled out. I didn't breathe or open my eyes until I pulled the door shut. My deprived lungs exploded as I heaved in gulp after gulp of fresh air. I placed my hands on my knees and panted.

The room was fuzzy, but I peered at the instructors from my hunched position. I panted, "I passed, right?"

"You're the first person to pass who hasn't come out of there with tears running down their face." The instructor's head tilted in curiosity. "How did you know to close your eyes?"

I stood up and stretched, the dizziness gone. "The vents. They have the smallest amount of yellow residue around the rims inside."

Godric leaned forward and placed his elbows on his knees. "I do have a question, Ms. Carvene."

"Okay." I eyed him with wariness.

"Do you have any suggestions on how to make it harder?"

My eyes widened in surprise. "Um...yes. If you switched the gas order, then it would be near impossible for someone to leave the room without tears."

He sat back in his chair and stared at the glass

room. "I'll speak with Mr. Cooper about it. Thank you for the suggestion."

I tipped my head. "You're welcome." Then I pointed inside the room. "Someone may want to call a medic. I hit him pretty hard."

Godric grunted. "Yes, we saw."

One male instructor groaned, disappointment in his eyes, staring at the prone body on the floor of the glass room. "What a shame. Victor had so much potential too."

I walked down the stairs with an extra pep in my step. "Not as much as me. Obviously."

CHAPTER TWENTY-SIX

Black hands with razor sharp nails swiped at my face.

I screeched and ducked.

Creatures with black leather skin and no eyes, their shape like humans surrounded the grassy field I stood on. Their numbers were as far as the eye could see, fanning the hill in their darkness. My bare toes dug into the dirt beneath, and my hands clenched into shaking fists.

I shouted, "What are you?"

The black creatures pulled closer.

Their mouths opened as wide as my head.

Neon green shone from within.

The light called to me.

I screamed...

My bedroom door slammed open.

I jerked up in my bed, my eyes flying wide. The blanket twisted around my legs, the soft sheet still clutched in my shaking fists against my chest. Sweat drenched my clothes and dampened my hair. I panted as my eyes darted from side to side, the sun almost rising—enough to light my room through the windows in a subdued glow.

Godric stormed past the entrance of my door that he had cracked in his haste to enter, his nostrils flared and his eyes alert as he scanned the small area. His navy blue pajama pants swooshed with each step he took, checking my bathroom and closet. The useless weapon he thought was dangerous was gripped in his right hand.

Finn stopped just inside my room.

He was only wearing his boxers.

Although, he did hold a wicked blade.

I panted and wiped the sweat from my forehead. The dream had been terrifying. I shook my head to dislodge the memory, my red hair whipping across my shoulders.

"What's wrong, Poppy?" Godric asked, his search done. The usual beautiful melody of his voice had disappeared, and in its place was a deadly cadence. He placed his weapon on my bedside, still close to him, and sat down on the edge of my bed. His hip pressed against mine. "Did someone break in?"

A delirious gurgle strangled my throat, the noise humiliating. I shook my head and answered breathlessly, "Other than you? No."

Finn turned and leaned outside my door, barking, "Get back to your rooms now."

Doors clicked shut all along the hall.

My cheeks instantly flushed with uncomfortable heat. I pulled the blanket back up to my chest, fidgeting with it. "Was I that loud?"

Godric tucked a stray strand of my hair behind my ear, his brutal golden eyes softening. "You were screaming."

Finn grunted.

I groaned and dropped my head.

Godric probed, "It was just a dream? No one tried to harm you here?"

"Just a dream," I mumbled. I kept my head down and rubbed at my forehead again. "A bad fucking dream."

He hummed on a quiet purr. "Do you want me to crawl in bed with you?"

Finn grumbled in amusement, "I'm out of here."

He shut the door as he left.

I tilted my head back up and stared at him with exasperation. "You cannot be in my bed. You need to follow your friend right on out of here."

His muscles clenched under his tan skin as he leaned toward me. He whispered, "Are you sure you want me to leave?"

No, I wanted him to stay and hold me tight.

"Yes, you need to." I flicked a finger at the door, attempting to gain a little control of the situation. "No matter what, this wouldn't look good if someone came through my door right now."

Godric's gaze ran over each of my features on my face, his eyes taking their time to evaluate me. "Do you want to talk about it?"

I shook my head. "It was just a fucking weird dream with black monsters. There wasn't any hidden meaning in it."

His head tilted. "Do you have many like that?"

I knew what he was asking.

"I don't have night terrors." There were plenty of individuals who did, though. The devastated world was too brutal in some areas, and it took a toll on people mentally. "But I have an occasional bad dream. That's all it was."

That appeased him.

Godric kissed my lips with a soft caress, and then he stood from my bed. He tucked his 'weapon' in the back of his pants at his waistline. "Try to get some rest. The instructors won't be up for a few more hours. We were up late until the last test was done."

I nodded.

But I stopped him when he reached the door.

"Godric?"

"Hmm?" He glanced back.

I stated softly, "Thank you."

His lips curved and his eyes sparkled. "My pleasure."

He shut the door silently as he left.

I stared at the long cracks in the wood.

That man I could get attached to.

And he was the last person I ever should.

* * *

I crept out of the Military House. The sun now showed on the horizon, lighting the front lawn in a simple, brilliant view that only occurs in the early morning hours. I pushed my hands into my pockets, a brisk chill in the air. It was a perfect day outside.

There was no way I could go back to sleep.

The dream still lingered in my mind and shivers continued to creep into my tense shoulders.

I trotted down the stairs and lifted my face to the sun, tipping my head back and closing my eyes. I breathed in the fresh air and relaxed my body, pushing away black monsters with gaping mouths. The birds were chirping their calls, and the city itself was quiet.

This is what I needed.

I put one foot in front of the other, strolling down the walkway to the fence. The gate was closed and locked. I couldn't leave, but it was a joy being outside.

I stared through the spaces of the wrought iron fence and examined each of the buildings across the street. They were new and colorful and were built strong when the rest of the world was still so torn.

The human race was rebuilding.

It just took so damn long.

I peered down in surprise when a particular stalker fox sat down on his haunches next to me. His eyes appraised the area as I had been doing. I shook my head, and muttered, "You have a real issue, mister. Stalking isn't polite."

He tipped his head back to look up at me.

His tongue lolled outside his mouth.

"Yeah, you're cute when you smile."

I sighed and sat down on the concrete walkway next to him. I lifted my hand very slowly, debated for a moment, and then touched the top of his head. His fur was soft under my fingers. The silver of his coat gleamed in the morning light. I dug my fingers in a little and scratched behind his ear.

He closed his eyes and tilted his head closer.

I snickered. "You're a weird fox."

His silver eyes opened. Barely.

My lips trembled. "You don't need to glare."

His expression didn't change.

"Okay. Okay. You're super cute too."

His tongue lolled out again.

I laughed loud and clear.

His furry head turned, and he licked my right cheek real quick. Then he sat back on his haunches again, all innocent. His tongue made another appearance as he grinned.

I snorted hard. "You're pretty sneaky too."

A throat cleared loudly.

I placed my right hand on the walkway behind me and twisted to see who was there.

Godric sat on the steps of the Military House—no clue how long he had been sitting there. He wore a pair of jeans and a simple t-shirt, his feet bare. His elbows rested on his bent knees, and his hands were clasped together. He was staring at the fox, no expression showing in his eyes.

He stated, "Get out of here."

His voice didn't rise. It was monotone.

My brows puckered. He was upset.

So upset he was hiding it behind a mask.

I shook my head. "He's not rabid."

Godric kept his eyes on the fox. "Now."

The fox instantly whined, but he dashed off.

He slid through one of the spaces in the fence. His tail whipped left and right as he ran down the middle of the street as fast as he could. He was just a streak of silver in the light before he disappeared completely around the end of the street.

I stood and brushed off the back of my pants. The

birds still chirped, and the sun was getting higher in the sky. I strolled back to the Military House and sat down on the steps. My right side pressed against Godric.

He was warm, but his muscles were tense.

My eyes evaluated his profile. "Know that fox?"

Godric still stared straight ahead, and he snorted. "That's a silly question, pet."

"Well, you're acting weird."

He ignored my comment. "I told you to get some rest."

"Sometimes I don't take orders well."

"And you're joining my army?"

"I said sometimes."

I turned my face back to the buildings across the street. Godric wasn't looking at me anyway, lost in his own thoughts. The magnificent buildings were all I could see.

I sighed in resignation, and muttered, "You built a beautiful city."

His laughter boomed. And it was extraordinary and resonated deep inside my chest, his foul mood broken. Godric leaned back and placed his left arm behind me on the stair above us. He peered at my profile this time.

"You sound thrilled."

I shrugged, my lips twitching in humor.

He whispered, "I won't tell your father you said that."

I groaned and dropped my head back. "And there you go ruining the moment. You had to bring up my father."

He chuckled, and his fingers started tracing circles on my lower back—a hidden caress. "My apologies, pet."

With my head still straight ahead, I peered at him out of the corner of my eye. "Is this why you had Theron watch over King Corporation? So you could be here with me?"

"That's part of the reason. I needed to see, with my own eyes, how you were doing or if you would be sent home to your father," he answered honestly, his voice intimate and quiet. "But I've also wanted to evaluate the instructors, see how they're handling new recruits. For the last two years, our numbers for acceptance into the CA haven't been as high as normal. But, so far, I'm pleased with the instructors' activities. It just appears those years were a weak bunch of recruits."

I leaned against his side a little more and turned my attention to him, staring into his fascinating eyes. "What will you do if I'm sent packing? It's not just my father I'll be going home to—it's also Brandon."

His nose scrunched. "I'm still debating on that."

I snickered. "You're adorable when you're confused."

"Am I?" he asked softly. He leaned forward just a touch, his heat enveloping my chilled frame. I shuddered in delight, and he smirked. "I'm not confused by one fact."

Always so arrogant.

"What's that?" I lifted my red brows.

"That I want you near me."

This was not where I'd thought he was going with this flirty line of conversation. I blinked in astonishment, and blabbered, "You can't just say that to me."

"Does that frighten you, pet?"

A little.

"No." I huffed. "But if I do have to go home, I won't live in New City. None of my father's soldiers do. Brandon certainly won't."

"You're correct about Mr. Moore." Those tiny circles he kept drawing on my back were so slow and lovely. "I believe General Carvene is grooming him to eventually take his place, so the next general would live primarily in Port, as is typical of the LA."

I had suspected as much.

I was like a torch passed down to the next leader of the Liberated Army, a prized filly for the great men who opposed the corporations.

My stomach churned at the thought.

"You don't like what I said."

I made a face at him. "Quit analyzing me."

He grinned, his eyes on my lips. "It comes naturally to me. I can't help it."

I peered back out at the buildings across the street.

He fully relaxed, staring at the sunrise.

We sat side-by-side in the early morning quiet.

It was incredibly peaceful.

Eventually, I whispered, "This is heading in a bad direction, Godric."

"I know," he stated smoothly. He continued to enjoy the view of the glorious sky. "I'll figure it out, though, pet. Just focus on passing the last test today. You're the only female remaining now."

CHAPTER TWENTY-SEVEN

The same male instructor was leading today. He stood at the front of the train while we sat in our seats like obedient little recruits, all eyes on him. There was only a total of forty-four remaining candidates. And it was judgment day.

"This is your final test. Half of you will be invited to the Corporate Army, half of you will go home with your tail between your legs." He said it all with a smile too. "Today, you will be tested on your strength and endurance. As soon as we arrive, you will participate in an obstacle course."

I was the smallest here.

This wasn't going to be fun.

"First, you will each cut down a tree in the designated area. Once you have finished with that, you will swim across the lake. There you will find an agility course. The first half of you to cross the finish line will pass." He was still grinning. "The rest of you will need to find your own mode of transportation back to the Military House to remove your belongings. If you don't pick up your items within twelve hours, they will be donated to the poor."

Okay. That was just mean.

He chuckled and took his seat where the rest of the instructors, along with Godric and Finn, sat at the front of the lavish train. The seven of them started chatting amongst themselves, enjoying the 'relaxing' train ride.

I closed my eyes and focused on my breathing.

Cut down a tree?

I'd never done that before in my life.

Swim across a lake?

I loved the water.

Agility course?

I was unsure. I would have to survey the terrain.

I really didn't want my ball cap, back in my room at the Military House, sent to the poor. But the odds today were a coin flip. I may end up having to steal my hat back from a destitute kid since I currently had no units for a train ride anywhere. If I failed, I would be stuck wherever the hell this train was taking us.

* * *

The train stopped, and the door opened automatically.

I shot from my seat in the middle of the train.

Only two others did the same.

The rest of the recruits watched in confusion.

But we had 'arrived,' the test now started.

I made it to the front of the train before the recruit in front of me turned and slammed his elbow right in the center of my chest. I stumbled back against a seat and grabbed at my shirt, my breath knocked out of me.

I choked, "You dumb motherfucker. A fight isn't how you're going to beat me today."

He smirked and turned to the door.

I shoved my hands back, my palms landing on a headrest and a person's head. I instantly knew it was Godric's head I was touching by the coarse curls beneath my fingers—and I was standing where the instructors still sat. I shoved off, hoping I didn't hurt him and jumped to the door.

I kicked Dumb Motherfucker right in his ass.

He flew out the door. "*Shit!*"

The bone in his right leg cracked when he landed on his side, his leg at an odd angle underneath him.

He shouted in instant pain, his face shading to a remarkable tomato red.

I grinned and hurried down the stairs. "Have fun losing today."

With my chest aching, I ran to a table where there were different types of equipment for chopping down a tree.

"Crap," I muttered. My hands fluttered over all them, unsure of what to pick. I had never used any of these before.

Well, I had trained with an ax before.

But I didn't think that was right.

The trees weren't huge before us in the roped area.

The other man, who had jumped up as the train door had opened too, stopped next to me. He took only a second, his gaze scanning before he grabbed a handsaw. Then he was running to the shoreline of the lake, to the trees there. This area would have been beautiful just to visit.

"Okay. Handsaw then."

I grabbed one of the five remaining handsaws on the table and a pair of the many safety gloves. Whoever was stuck with the metal nail files in the center of the table was screwed. I ran down the hill as all the other recruits were shoving each other to get out of the train. Dumb Motherfucker was still moaning on the ground and recruits had to jump over him, dust flying up in his damp face.

I sprinted to stand next to the guy with the other handsaw. I wasn't above learning while I worked. The way he was holding it made sense, and I positioned my gloved hands the same way. He breathed out every time he sawed, so I did the same.

The train lifted into the air, the blue glow shining below it as it traveled over the lake to the finish line. I didn't see any instructors nearby—or even Godric or Finn—so they were probably on the train.

Though, there were a few medics close-by.

I was sure they would be busy today.

CHAPTER TWENTY-EIGHT

What I didn't get right in my task, as sweat poured down my face, was the extra notch I should have cut into the tree. Halfway through the tree, with my shoulder muscles aching, my saw was hardly cutting through it anymore. I stopped and stood, wiping sweat from my forehead with the back of my gloved hand.

I shook my head in frustration.

Then I merely walked over to the guy's tree next to me and watched him work. He didn't seem to mind. He glanced at me once and went back to hacking away at the tree.

"Fuck," I complained, bending down to stare at the angled notch. That was just as much work as what I'd already accomplished. "I have to do that too?"

He grunted and kept sawing.

A guy ran by and rushed into the lake.

"That's not good," I mumbled.

My feet were in motion, running back to my tree.

I worked faster, my muscles screaming in pain.

The sun peeked in the sky, but the shaking leaves of the trees shaded everyone remaining—though the body heat that poured off my body was brutal, my white shirt soaked through. I was extremely happy I had worn a sturdy thick bra today.

More men ran by to the cool water of the lake.

And my goddamn tree finally fell.

I hurried to cut the remaining bits still attached to the trunk, and then I dropped the handsaw and my safety gloves on the ground. My palms were still red, but the protective gloves had done their job.

The guy who had been next to me was already across the lake and running up the shoreline to the agility course.

My boots trampled the grass as I charged to the lake. I debated removing them, but I had no idea what the agility course was. There could be glass to walk on for all I knew. So I dove into the water once I was waist deep—boots and all.

The water was refreshing, but I was exhausted.

I turned onto my back. I used the backstroke to swim across the lake. It actually loosened my tight muscles, and I ended up passing two men in the water—though, there were still a lot ahead of me. I had lost count of who had finished cutting down their trees before I had.

I turned in the water when pebbles brushed underneath my fingers. The rocks were slippery, so I was careful as I scrambled out of the water and onto the shoreline. My boots were waterlogged. If I didn't need them on the agility course, I was going to ditch them in a hurry.

I wiped lake water off my face as I came to a halt where the last task began. I stared at the massive red wall before me with tiny fake rocks sticking out for hand and foot holds. It was like rock climbing. I had done that with my father as a child when we would go hiking, but it had been years since my last time. However, I did remember one important point of it.

I had to be able to reach the first hold.

The instructors were sitting on folding chairs in the shade to my left, which meant the course wasn't long. They sat silently and watched the proceedings. Close to fifteen recruits were sitting behind them on the grass, already done—lucky sons-of-bitches.

And there were a whole lot more in front of me

145

fighting on the wall or at the bottom of it. It didn't bode well for me at all.

I quickly ditched my boots and socks and ran to the wall. But I stayed back a few feet from the fray of flying fists. Bodies dropped from the wall directly on top of the fighters, only for it to start all over again. It was a goddamn heartless mess.

The first hold was too high for me to reach by myself. I could tell that easily from where I stood. I nibbled on my bottom lip and walked back and forth from one end to the other. All of them were too high.

"That is not fair," I griped under my breath.

No one was going to give me a boost.

I eyed the fighting men in front of me.

No, they definitely wouldn't help.

My eyes narrowed on the two men at the end.

Perhaps they could help.

They just didn't know they were going to...yet.

I backed up on quick feet and shook out my arms.

I had to do this super-fast or I was screwed.

Then I moved.

I raced as hard as I could with my arms pumping and my bare feet digging down into the ground. The two men had hold of each other's heads, bent over each other as they pounded one another in the stomachs. They didn't even notice me coming. I jumped into the air and scrambled up on top of them. They both jerked up in surprise, and I leapt with my arms extended upward and snagged a hold.

My body smacked against the wall.

I groaned from the pain but quickly heaved my right leg up to a hold on the right. One of the men grabbed at my dangling left leg, cursing at me, but I kicked him straight in his throat. He fell back on his ass unable to breathe.

The other guy took advantage of his rival falling and jumped to grab a hold next to me.

I eyed the recruit as I heaved and flew up to the next hold, my fingers digging into it. I asked in a breathless pant, "Are you going to fuck with me?"

His muscles bulged as he used just his arms to toss himself up next to me again. "I've seen you fight. I'll leave you alone."

I still watched him.

Near the top of our severe climb, I muttered, "You've got incoming below you."

He glanced down. "Thanks."

Then he kicked his foot hard into a man's face.

The poor bastard fell backward through the air.

I looked away, not wanting to see the landing.

We were up high at this point.

The wind whipped my ponytail as I stopped to catch my breath for a second. My muscles quivered, and my fingers were shaking. I grunted and dug my toes better into the hold below me, pressing my body flat against the wall. I twisted my wrists to stretch my fingers.

I heaved myself one more time and slapped a hand down on top of the wall, a husky bellow passed my lips as I pulled my aching and exhausted body up with the last of my strength. I sucked oxygen for a second, lying on my back, and staring up at the blue sky, the sun beginning its descent.

"Get up," I hissed to myself.

I rolled and stood to my feet, preparing myself for more hell. But I stared at the finish line down below. It was right there. And there was only one more step I needed to take.

I sat down at the back edge of the wall and pushed.

I tucked my arms in as my body flew down the slide.

Then I was clawing at the ground and thrusting myself up to my feet. The man I had helped slid down next to me, still lying on his back. I stared down at him for a second, his gaze freezing on mine in his prone position. I could kick him and debilitate him.

I chose not to.

I sprinted across the grass as fast as I could, my chest heaving and my arms pumping by my sides. His feet pounded behind me, gaining on my position. My mouth opened, and I squealed in excitement with a victory punch in the air, my tiny feet passing the white line painted on the grass.

CHAPTER TWENTY-NINE

I stopped and sucked air as I punched my fist into the air again with a little hop. I looked back at the guy, and he was grinning too as he fell onto the grass and lay flat on his back, his arms spread wide.

I hissed, "We did it!"

There weren't over twenty recruits sitting behind the instructors—only nineteen. We had just made the cut.

"To not killing each other." He held his hand up into the air for me to high-five.

I smacked his hand in giddy delight. "To not killing each other." My smile had to gleam in the sunlight. "What's your name?"

"Ben Prac."

"I'm Poppy Carvene."

He snorted. "I know who you are."

One more man crossed the finish line behind us.

The instructors instantly stood to their feet.

Recruits resting behind them followed their lead.

Godric was watching me under hooded eyelids, a tiny smile curling his lips. He winked at me in private congratulations. Godric the Great appeared damn pleased that I had passed.

My grin was glorious. I had done it!

Ben lifted his hand from his horizontal spot on the grass, muttering, "Give me a hand up, yeah?"

I grabbed his hand and yanked him to his feet.

Then I froze as a silent man came out of the tree

line behind the train. He wore a silver fur hooded coat with the hood up over his head. Silver hair stuck out from under it in chaotic strands. He had a black pair of leather pants on and a white t-shirt. Two swords were crossed against his back, the black handles seen above his shoulders. There were no shoes on his feet.

He stalked right toward me.

I turned to him with wariness. I didn't know him.

His eyes were the color of shining silver blades.

Ben mumbled, "Who the fuck is that?"

Godric and Finn charged by us, marching at a fast clip toward the stranger. They didn't have weapons in their hands, but their shoulders were tight with tension as they stopped in front of him.

Godric growled, "You are not wanted here."

Silver eyes didn't flinch, his tone bored. "Oh, you'll want me here, God."

My head cocked with the use of his nickname.

Finn held his hands up between the two. "Let's take this discussion somewhere else." His head snapped to the newcomer. "That is if you came here for a reason, Cassander? Not just to piss him off?"

Cassander with the silver eyes yawned. "Of course, I came here for a reason. I wouldn't show up after all these years without one." He looked between the two of them, straight at me. He tipped his head in my direction and then pointed an accusing gaze on Godric. "I came to protect her."

Godric's eyes narrowed. His fists clenched.

Finn's head darted back and forth between the two of them, and then he speared the silver-eyed man with a look. "Quit fucking around, Cass. He's about to snap."

Cassander's lips tilted up. "Fine. I am here to protect her. But not from the asshole across from me."

"What are you talking about?" Godric growled.

Cassander lifted his hands above his head and drew his swords, the sun bouncing off the metal in a brilliant gleam. He tipped his head back toward the wooded area he had come from. "We're about to have company."

Godric's gaze slammed toward the trees, and his nostrils flared. He stepped forward, his eyes trained on the tree line. His voice was whisper quiet, deadly, and fierce. "Finn, get everyone out of here."

Finn was already walking away. "On it."

Ben leaned toward me, also staring at the trees. "Were they talking about you?"

"I think," I mumbled in confusion.

There were bigger problems than that right now.

I quickly trotted across the grass to stand next to Godric as the instructors and Finn herded recruits into the train. "Are we about to be attacked or something?"

"Yes," Cassander and Godric stated together.

I snapped my attention to the trees. "By who?"

Godric's nostrils were still flared. "I don't know."

"Not by who," Cassander drawled. "By *what*."

I stood on the grassy field with bare feet.

And I froze.

Black creatures with razor sharp nails were creeping closer to the edge of the tree line, moving as if they were floating, with no particular straight pattern as they crossed in front of each other and back again. They moved so slowly that a one-legged dog could beat them in a race.

My hands shook down by my sides. "Someone pinch me. I'm dreaming again." I wanted to wake up now.

"Not a dream," Cassander murmured.

Neither of the two took their eyes from the monsters.

Finn shoved the last of the recruits, who had made it to this side of the lake, inside the train, then barked at the instructors, "Hurry the fuck up, people."

They ran inside, the confusion evident on their faces why they were leaving in such a hurry. But they obeyed the orders and raced up the stairs, disappearing inside.

My shoulders stiffened. "We need to get on that

train." I grabbed Godric's hand with my shaking ones. "Come on, big man. Let's go."

"Finn, get Poppy on there!" Godric ordered.

But the door on the train shut on its own.

The train lifted into the air and shot over the lake.

I trembled where I stood, my lips quivering.

Godric bellowed, "What the fuck, Finn! She can't be here."

Finn jogged to our small group. He shook his head, his eyes wide in shock and confusion. "I didn't do that."

"I snuck in there earlier and set the timer." Cassander yawned again. "Because she can be here."

"Are you crazy?" I screamed. I pointed at the monsters heading toward us. "I don't *want* to be here for whatever the hell you guys are up to."

Cassander sighed. "Ms. Carvene, take the knife that God's hiding against his right ankle."

"I don't want a weapon. I want to leave."

"Just take it out."

I ground my teeth together.

Nevertheless, I bent and grabbed the knife that was indeed hidden under Godric's pant leg. I straightened with the polished blade in my hand. "It's pretty. But I still want to go. Call the train back, someone."

Cassander snickered. "Do me one more favor."

"What?" I snapped.

"Prick the tip of God's thumb with the blade."

Godric blinked. He didn't breathe.

"I'm not going to cut him."

"Just a tiny prick. Then I'll call the train back."

I grabbed Godric's closest hand and pressed the tip of the blade to his finger. "Sorry about this, big man. But that guy is crazy, and we need to get the hell out of here."

Godric didn't move a muscle as I put a little pressure on the knife. His eyes did lower though from the tree line to stare at his finger. A drop of blood beaded on his skin.

I pulled the knife away, and ordered, "Call it."

Finn stared at the blood. He reached forward and brushed his finger over Godric's, wiping the dot away.

Another blood dot formed slowly.

Finn choked. "Oh my. Fuck, God."

Godric swayed where he stood, still staring at his finger. He whispered, "I don't understand."

"Neither do I," I groused. I put a hand on his shoulder since it appeared he was about to faint at the sight of his own blood. "I want to get the hell out of here. And your friend is a liar."

Godric argued absently, "He's not my friend."

He wiped off the blood, pinched his thumb, and stared in a daze as another blood drop beaded on his skin.

"Jesus, quit doing that. You look faint enough." I rubbed his shoulder. Hard. "Godric, snap out of it. I'm seriously freaking out. The monsters from my nightmare are coming this way, and I'm afraid I'm either dead from the last test, have hit my head, or I've been drugged. I want to leave. Please."

"You're not any of those things, Ms. Carvene." Cassander snickered, and then lowered his swords. He placed them on the ground. "This is so anticlimactic. The bastard must be weak. Those things are a lot slower than I thought they'd be. I imagined I'd rush to the rescue and get to kill some bad guys, but instead, they are slower than snails. Seriously. I've seen snails move faster than those rickety ass bad guys."

"Call the train," I hissed.

He ignored me. "I've got time to explain something."

Then he did the unexpected.

I shook Godric's shoulder again, my eyes widening in surprise. "Godric... Your crazy friend is stripping in front of us."

"Not my friend," he mumbled again.

Godric the Great stared at the tiny bead of blood.

"You're not impressing me right now, big man."

Finn blinked out of his own lethargy. "Just give

him a minute, Poppy. He'll be back to his controlling self in no time. Probably a whole lot more with you once he gets his shit together."

"Watch it, asshole."

"See? He's already getting better."

They were all losing it.

Cassander dropped his pants on top of the other clothes he had removed. He wasn't wearing underwear.

I blinked at the naked man.

The pretty, pretty naked man.

Cassander lifted a finger. "Watch."

"Call the damn train!"

"Don't blink," he ordered.

I froze in place, my mind instantly reeling.

White sparkles twisted like a tornado where he had stood, his body gone from sight.

"What?" I whispered, choking on air.

The tornado of sparkles disappeared.

A silver stalker fox sat on his haunches, and his tongue lolled out in a grin—where Cassander used to be.

I dropped the knife as my eyelashes fluttered.

"Someone, catch me," I breathed.

The landscape sloped as I tipped to the side, my eyes closing on their own. Godric's arms wrapped around me right before I hit the ground and the world ceased to exist.

CHAPTER THIRTY

"Where are we going?" I asked softly, my arms wrapped around my stomach. My reality had changed when I'd woken up surrounded by monsters with their heads torn off.

Godric, Finn, and Cassander had killed them all.

Then a freaking train had arrived.

A private King Corporation train.

The clean blue energy vibrated under my bare feet.

Godric didn't speak, his attention steadfast outside the window, with his chin resting on his fist.

After they had finished fighting, he carried me into the train, placed me on a chair, and wrapped a blanket around my shivering form. But he hadn't said a word.

Apparently, he still wasn't talking.

Finn cleared his throat after looking at his friend, the mute man. "I believe our destination is Godric's home."

I swallowed and finally looked at Cassander.

I whispered, "Did you really turn into a..."

His smile was gentle. "A fox. I shift into a fox."

The air rushed out of my lungs in a shaky exhale. "What are you exactly?"

His brows rose, and he flicked his finger at Godric and Finn. "Don't you mean, what are *we*?"

155

My jaw went slack in fear, and my voice was shrill. "All three of you turn into a fox?"

"No." Cassander smirked. "I'm the only fox in this room."

My brows furrowed as my gaze flicked back and forth between Finn and Godric. "What do you two turn into?"

Finn's eyes didn't leave mine. "I'm a white tiger."

I pushed myself back against my seat.

"Lion," Godric murmured absently.

The hair on the back of my neck stood up, and a horrible shiver plagued my frame. My teeth started chattering. When Godric had finally decided to speak, he destroyed my sanity.

I shook my fist at him. "I'm living in a different reality right now, and you are being an asshole. I need some goddamn comfort. It's not everyday nightmares become real, and humans become animals."

Godric sat back in his chair and turned his attention to me. His golden eyes pinned my shaking form in place. "We aren't human, Poppy."

I pulled the blanket tighter around my shoulders and eyed him even more warily. "Are you an alien?"

"No, we're called shifters. We don't just turn into an animal. The animal is part of who we are, so we're able to shift at will."

I hissed, "I fucked a lion?"

His eyes narrowed. "You fucked me."

"You just said the animal is part of who you are."

"I meant, in this form, we have certain traits that our animal counterpart has. Most shifters hear better than you can imagine. We can see better than any human in the dark. Our sense of smell is off the charts. And our personalities tend to shadow how our animal would act in the wild—but that's not always the case."

"You said 'most' shifters." I eyed him hard. "How many shifters are there?"

"A lot."

"How much is a lot?"

"Roughly thirty percent of the world's male population."

I could only stare.

He snorted, peering down his nose. "You humans killed each other off. That wasn't our doing. It's the shifters now who are trying to keep your race from complete annihilation."

I nibbled on my bottom lip.

Something was off there.

"Why would shifters care if humans exist? Wouldn't it be easier if we didn't?"

His jaw clenched. He peered back out the window.

Finn's lips curved. "You're very intelligent, Poppy."

Godric grunted, his eyes staying on the scenery.

Cassander sat forward and placed his elbows on his knees. "We need humans because shifters are all males. Our mates are human."

"Mates?" My brows creased.

"A mate is chosen by magic. A perfect counterpart to their shifter male. But the shifter doesn't know who the person is until after they have sex and a test is done."

"So shifters are magic?"

"Yes."

"What kind of test does a shifter perform on an unsuspecting human after sex? You would want to know, so I imagine you do it every time, right?"

"We do. And it's very simple."

"What?"

"Another shifter pricks their hand. If it heals instantly, then they are an actual mate to whoever they slept with."

"Magic makes it heal?" I was catching on.

"Yes. Shifters and mates are immortal."

I sucked in a lungful of oxygen. "You can't *die*?"

Cassander peered down at his hands and picked at his leather pants. "There are two ways a shifter can die. One is their mate kills them. The other is the seer kills them."

"What's a seer?"

He cleared his throat. "There's only one seer alive at one time. The seer has special abilities. But the seer's primary job is for killing. If there's a shifter who goes insane over time, the seer takes him out. Or if a mate or shifter want their existence gone—forever is a long time to live—then the seer performs an investigation to see if it is for the best and handles it accordingly."

Godric growled deep in his throat.

I glanced at him but quickly peered back to the man giving me all the answers. "Does a shifter actually need a 'mate'?"

Cassander was right.

Forever was a long time to be with someone.

"Yes. They are the only people we can breed with."

I blinked, finally getting there. "That's why the shifters are really helping to save the human race. It saves them from extinction."

Finn smirked. "Bingo."

My eyes slowly squinted in distrust. "Wait. You said you're immortal. If you're immortal, then you heal fast, right?"

Cassander nodded, still picking at his pants. "We do. Heads grow back. Hearts grow back. Even if we're burned down to ash, we form again."

I snorted. "Then why didn't Godric's finger heal?"

The train went completely silent.

"So you're lying to me," I accused.

"We've told you the truth. You just haven't put it all together yet." Godric turned his stunning eyes on me, his gaze unwavering now. "The reason why a different shifter has to perform the test on the human is that a mate's shifter or a shifter's mate can physically hurt each other. The test would read that the human wasn't a mate if her sex partner did it since a mate's shifter can hurt them. They wouldn't heal."

I blinked.

Stared. Trembled.

Almost hyperventilated.

I choked, "What are you saying?"

Godric's golden eyes didn't falter. "You're my mate."

My hand shot out in front of Cassander. "Cut my finger."

Godric hissed through his clenched teeth.

Cassander closed his eyes and rubbed his forehead.

Finn pulled out his knife with a long sigh. "Give me your hand."

"Why not him? He's obviously a shifter." I glared, my body trembling in shock at Godric's declaration. "I've seen him shift, not you."

Finn explained calmly, "Cassander is our seer. It won't work with him." He flicked his free hand at me. "Now give me your hand so you can see the truth and start to process it all."

My nostrils flared in suspicion, but I placed my trembling hand in front of him. "Fine."

His blade flashed so fast I barely saw it.

As in, a human can't move that fast.

I flinched at the sting. "Ow!"

Godric growled. It wasn't human. There was a lion's growl coming from inside his chest. He hissed, "You cut too deep."

"I apologize, but she needed to feel it."

I jerked my full gaze from Godric, swallowing down the hysteria choking me from the noise he made and peered down at my hand. There was a line of blood on my palm, and a cut down into the flesh. But, as I watched, my skin knit itself together so fast, I would have missed it if I'd blinked.

I wiped the blood on the blanket.

My body started trembling for a new reason.

I jerked my attention to the man with the golden lion eyes. My chest heaved as I burned inside. "You didn't tell me."

"I didn't know," Godric growled. He leaned forward in his seat, his gaze fueled with fury. "One of my guards was supposed to check after you left the bedroom, but you evaded them. So I sent Jonathan after you. That bastard lied to me. He said you tested negative."

Finn whistled. "Oh shit."

"I'm fucking burying him."

The fight instantly died within me. "I evaded him too. That wasn't his fault. He was probably scared to tell you."

"He lied to me." Godric seethed, his cheeks flushing with anger. "Shifters do not take a mate test lightly. It is our existence, as you stated. I will bury that bastard. And I'll enjoy it."

"Godric..." I reprimanded gently.

"What would you have done if your whole life, your *entire* immortal life, you never understood why you couldn't die. Why you never aged. Why you had to suffer watching friends grow old and die over and over again...*forever*."

My mouth shut. I shivered in fear.

"Exactly. The bastard will be buried."

I held his furious gaze.

So many thoughts poured through my head.

My top emotion was fear, my back tense with it.

I asked softly, "Why was Cassander following me?"

"Because he knew."

"And he didn't tell you?"

He hissed, "The seer keeps many secrets."

I peered in Cassander's direction where he still had his eyes closed and was continually massaging his forehead. "Your job sucks, Cassander."

Under his rubbing hand, silver eyes peeked open. "That is an understatement."

CHAPTER THIRTY-ONE

Godric clamped his hand down on my shoulder, keeping me steady on my feet as we exited the train. "Are you going to faint again?"

I shook my head. "No."

The world and my life had altered in the matter of a few hours—but I was made of stronger stuff. My father's genes were potent, and I had them in spades. The existence in which I lived may have transformed, but I would roll with it. I wouldn't be trampled on by the truth.

We stopped just outside the train to wait for Cassander and Finn. They were talking inside the transport, giving Godric and me a moment of privacy.

I stared at Godric's house before me.

It was a mansion of white stucco with a red tiled roof constructed on a rocky outcrop, the land reminiscent of a peninsula with ice blue water surrounding it on three sides.

My eyebrows lifted gradually. I didn't peek up at him as I spoke, but my eyes remained trained on where he lived.

"You're a lion, right?"

"A lion shifter," he clarified.

His hand was still tense on my shoulder.

The man had effectively shut down again after all the details of who and what they were had finished on our ride.

I cleared my throat. "Then why do you choose to live here? It doesn't look like a place a lion would hunker down. There aren't any trees or sand or tall grass nearby—and it's so open."

The area was beautiful, but not wild.

"Really?" he asked in a dry tone.

"What?" I shrugged. "If I were a lion, I wouldn't live here."

"I'm also a man, Poppy."

"So, you like this then?"

"It's a little extravagant, but yes. I do like it."

I nibbled on my bottom lip. "Why am I here?"

He didn't answer, his hand tightening on my shoulder. His massive body crept behind me. The heat flowing off him was delicious, but he was still intimidating.

"Godric, answer my question."

He bent and placed his lips against my left ear, and whispered, "Do you want to run away? Because I would probably enjoy that. I adore a great chase."

I ground my teeth together. "You have to ask if you want me to stay here. You can't just cart me off to your home and expect me to be okay with it."

I would have said yes.

He still needed to ask, though.

"I never wanted a mate, Poppy. I've been abstinent from sex for over a hundred years because I didn't want one. While I may not be entirely thrilled with this development right now, I won't run from it. Now that I have a mate, you aren't going anywhere. Especially when there's evil lurking after you. I protect what is mine."

My mouth bobbed. I didn't know where to begin with all the information Godric had just spewed. In the end, I shook my head, and muttered, "How old are you?"

"Almost two hundred." His lips grazed my ear.

I blinked and set aside the fact he had been alive before the war had torn the world apart. "You weren't abstinent for the first hundred years of your life, were you? That means you didn't mind if you found a mate back then. What made you change your mind a hundred years ago?"

His lips curved against the edge of my ear. "I do like that I have a cunning mate." He inhaled deeply, smelling my hair. "The last six mate pairings weren't right. As in, there was something wrong with the magic. That had never happened before. The magic was off. It was tainted with darkness."

"Oh." I pressed my body closer to him as a chilly breeze ruffled my hair. "Is this...pairing...between us wrong?"

"I don't scent any darkness around you." He inhaled deeply again, and his voice lowered to pure intimacy. "I only smell a woman I'd love to fuck."

My throat went dry. "Do many women smell like that to you?"

His lips twitched as he wrapped his arms around my waist from behind and held me tight against his body. He set his chin on top of my head, staring at the water. "Is that jealousy I hear?"

Maybe a little.

"Not at all." I cleared my throat. "Answer my question, please."

His chest rumbled against my back. "I can honestly tell you that no woman has ever smelled as appealing as you do. You broke my abstinence, pet. I didn't give a fuck about the consequences. I wanted to bend you over and screw you right there on the bar."

My lower gut fanned with sensual flame. This mate business frightened me, but I offered, "You smell good too."

His chest started to shake in silent humor.

"What? You do." Dammit, it was a compliment.

"Tell me what your little human nose smells."

"Wildness and spice with a hint of cherries."

He bellowed with his laughter, my body shaking with his inside his protective hold. "That is precious, pet."

"Don't laugh at me," I groused. "I don't have a lion sniffer. But you still smell good."

"It's kind of cute, really." He was returning to himself now, no longer the man holding everything in and shutting out the people around him. "Cherries, you said?"

I turned my head under his chin and sniffed his shoulder. "Yeah, it's still there. Nice and sweet. Is it your shampoo or soap?"

He muttered, "I would never use anything that made me smell like a cherry."

"Then it's just you."

He snorted. "Or you have a fucked up nose."

"Are you offended you smell sweet?"

He sniffed, not commenting.

I grinned. "Don't worry, big man. I like it."

Finn and Cassander exited the train, not bothering to hide the fact they weren't exactly human. They didn't take the stairs. The two just jumped out the door, flying through the air toward us.

Cassander's long fur jacket blew out behind him and whooshed forward as he landed in a crouch. He stood, his attention on Godric, his silver eyes narrowed. "Are you going to let me in your home so we can talk about what happened today? Or are you going to continue to be an asshole, and make me wait on the lawn?"

Finn ran a hand through his white hair. "Cass, can you try to be halfway civil?"

Cassander snorted. "Go stick yourself with a blade, Finn. I am being civil right now." Silver eyes turned to the man holding me close, waiting for an answer.

The rough waves lapped at the rocky shore.

"Cassander is the only one who knew the monsters were coming. It only makes sense to talk with him about it." I tipped my head to the side and peered back. "Godric, why won't you let him into your home?"

The other two looked away.

Godric raised one eyebrow. He answered simply, no inflection in his tone. "Because Cassander killed my mother. She was one of the six wrong pairings, and he chopped off her head when she asked him to do it."

CHAPTER THIRTY-TWO

"Oh," I whispered softly.

Cassander picked at his fur coat, not speaking.

"Well, I..." I cleared my throat, my voice too breathless from shock. I shook my head and aligned my thoughts. "Didn't you tell me you value intelligence? No matter who it comes from? It might be a good time to heed your own words."

Godric's nostrils flared, staring down into my eyes. "I've changed my mind. Having a cunning mate is annoying."

My red brows lifted. I waited.

Godric knew what the right call was.

The lion—the freaking lion—growled softly in his throat. Then he pierced the seer with a death glare. "I'll let you inside. This one time."

Cassander continued to mess with his coat, rumbling with a light tone, "How very kind of you, God. I'm so happy to accept your fine invitation into your home. I'm sure I'll have the most wonderful time."

It hit me then. I had thought it interesting before. But only his friends called him by that nickname.

These two had been close once.

I glanced back and forth between them.

Their eyes shuttered all true feelings as we started walking down the paved walk to the mansion on the water.

They had been friends. Perhaps the closest.

That was why they were in such pain.

One hid it with anger. The other with humor.

The four of us walked up the white marble stairs that opened to a massive marble porch. There were many cushioned, comfortable seats as if he had company over a lot. Potted trees were placed next to the seats for an interesting form of shade to use in the daytime sun. It brought a little of the forest to his home.

I stopped dead in my tracks and stared.

Then I laughed, holding my stomach. "Oh my goodness. You are so vain."

Godric peered down his nose. "It's expensive."

"And that makes it any better?" I waved my hands in front of the enormous statue right next to his front door. "Is this what you look like when you shift?"

"Yes. Alaric crafted it for me."

It was a lion. One big ass golden lion.

I knocked on it. "Wait. Is this real gold?"

"I said it was expensive." He shrugged and unlocked his door, holding it open for us. His brows lowered in thought. "We should probably call the rest of the group. And my father."

"Do we really need to bring your father into this?" Finn complained as he walked inside. "We can try to handle this on our own first."

Cassander rolled his eyes and turned his body so he wasn't close to his old friend as he slid inside. "The man is ancient. If anyone has any advice to give, it'll be him."

I still stared at the statue.

"Are you coming, Poppy?" Godric probed.

I shook my head at the waste of money on such a frivolous item and walked into his home. "I'm going to put a pink sparkly bow around that lion's neck. That is how ridiculous that monstrosity is."

"Touch it, and I'll spank you." Godric crossed his arms.

My eyes narrowed on his. "You wouldn't dare."

"Try me." His gaze ran over my features, and then he walked away through the gigantic foyer. Over his shoulder, he asked, "Where do we want to talk? Office or living room?"

My bracelet buzzed. I glanced down and read the readout. Oh, this will be fun. I cleared my throat, and stated, "Actually, I need to take this call first."

The three men stopped and looked back.

Godric asked, "Who is it?"

"My father." I tapped my bracelet, putting him on hold. I looked up, keeping my expression serene. "Is there a place I can talk in private?"

Godric ground his molars together. "You and I will need to discuss your father at some point."

Because I was his...mate.

This situation was fucked.

"We will talk." I waved my hand left and right. "But where do I go to take this?"

He pointed to my left. "The kitchen is down that hallway. It's private enough. Eat something while you talk with him. You look exhausted."

I nodded and started that way. "I will. Thank you."

"And Poppy?" Godric purred.

I stopped and looked at him. "Yeah?"

One side of his lips curled up into a cruel smile. "Make sure to tell your father you're no longer marrying Mr. Moore. However you want to phrase it, I don't care. Because if Mr. Moore comes to New City to claim you, I will kill him."

* * *

"Hello, Father." I popped a handful of nuts into my mouth, chewing vigorously. My left foot kept tapping in my nervousness, and my palms were sweating. "How are you doing?"

"Poppy Bree Carvene, I am so upset with you," he growled. My full name had been used. He was well and truly pissed. "Did you even think before you ran away? Or did you merely not give a shit about what I thought was best for you?"

I closed my eyes and dropped my forehead into my right hand. "I love you, Father. I do care what you think. But I told you so many times I wasn't going to marry a stranger. You didn't listen to *me*."

"So you just decided the fucking Corporate Army was the best solution?" He grunted over the call. "You're lucky I covered for you when they contacted me. Otherwise, you'd be sitting in a jail cell right now, darling dearest."

"I'm sorry. I really am."

He was quiet for a long second before he asked, "The tests should be done by now. Do I need to send a train to pick you up and bring you home? Or did those cocksuckers get their claws into you?"

A genuine smile lifted my lips. I tossed a couple more nuts into my mouth with glee. I whispered in excitement, "I passed, Father. I did really well."

"Of course, you did. You're my kid."

I grinned full-blown. "You're proud of me. I can hear it in your voice."

"Those tests are rough. That signature you forged of mine was allowing your death sentence. I obtained a copy of it, and there's a goddamn death clause in it stating they aren't responsible if you die during their tests."

"Well, I didn't die." I cleared my throat.

I would never die now.

My head spun again with the realization.

"But you could have."

"I'm fine," I lied. I shook my head past the dizziness, and put my new life existence on the backburner. "So about Brandon..."

My father snorted. "I'll handle him."

"Are you sure?"

"You're staying in that damn Corporate Army, aren't you?"

"Yes."

"Then the marriage contract is void."

I took another drink of water. "Father, I think he kind of liked me. He kissed my hand for a long time."

"Wait, did you like him too? Am I misreading this?"

"No. I didn't like him. What I'm trying to say is that I don't want him coming after me."

There was a smile in his voice. "Don't worry, darling dearest. Your father will handle the big scary man for you."

I chuckled. "Don't kill him."

"I won't," he hummed. "As long as he doesn't mess with you. I don't think he will. As I said before, he's a good man. And he's one I trust. But I've seen good men turn bad too. I'll keep an eye on him."

I sighed. "Father, I really am sorry."

He rumbled, "For which thing? That you joined Mr. King's army or for turning your back on the Liberated Army or for running away and making me worry you might die?"

I nibbled on my bottom lip. "It's not as bad as all that."

"It's exactly like that." His sigh was loud. "But, contrary to popular opinion—I'm talking about your opinion—I do understand why you did it."

"Seriously?"

He chuckled. "Back in the day, I was once young. I know what it's like to be forced into marriage. Though, I was lucky. Your mother and I came to love each other very much."

I grinned. "I can see why. You're quite the catch."

"Maybe a long time ago I was."

I popped another nut into my mouth. "You still are. I got my looks from you. And you always say I'm too pretty for my own good." I chewed in thought. "You know, Father, since you like those marriage contracts so much, you could always sign yourself up again—"

171

"No!" he cut me off fast. Then he breathed and stated more calmly, "Don't be cheeky."

I laughed in pure malicious entertainment. "You don't like those tables being turned on you, huh?"

"Hush," he muttered. "So when can I see you?"

"Miss me already?"

"What I don't miss is your dishes left everywhere. It's been nice having a clean kitchen."

I glanced at all of the food I had scattered over Godric's kitchen counter. His pantry was stuffed with so many items that I'd just grabbed whatever looked good. I would have to clean the mess up after I finished eating.

"So when can I see you?" my father pestered.

My eyes narrowed at his tone. "Everything all right?"

He was quiet for too long.

"Father?"

"Actually, Poppy, I received an interesting photo of you. I'd like to talk to you about it in person, not like this."

"What kind of photo?" I asked cautiously.

My bracelet buzzed. I tapped on it.

A hologram picture formed in front of me.

"That photo," my father said, his voice quiet.

I sucked in a harsh breath.

The fear of it being a photo of Godric and me on the front lawn of King Corporation vanished. It was much worse than us sitting side-by-side in the grassy courtyard eating lunch together. This photo was intimate and left nothing to the imagination.

Godric's beautiful naked flesh was on full display from the backside. He was on his knees on the bed, his face tilted to the side showing his profile. And he had me pinned to the headboard, my head thrown back in ecstasy with my bare limbs wrapped around his body.

My father cleared his throat. "That is Mr. King, correct?"

"Yes," I croaked, my voice filled with guilt.

"And that is a bedroom on my base. Correct?"

I whispered, "Yes."

He stopped speaking, quiet. So quiet.

I didn't know what to say, so I stayed silent.

We didn't speak for a full minute.

Then it only became worse.

Godric walked into the kitchen on silent feet, griping in exasperation, "Poppy, everyone is arriving. If you're done eating, we need to start discussing what happened today."

But he jerked to a stop, his eyes caught on the photo before me. The man blinked slowly. His head cocked as he evaluated the picture, his eyes narrowing in slow cooking fury.

Then he bellowed, "What the fuck is that?"

My eyes were wide on my face. "Godric, wait. My father—"

"I don't give a damn about your father right now," he interrupted. He stormed forward and pointed at the photo. "How the hell do you have a picture of us like this? No one was in the room then."

My mouth bobbed, horror etching my features.

My father cleared his throat. "That's Mr. King, I presume, Poppy?"

CHAPTER THIRTY-THREE

Godric's shoulders tensed and his attention snapped to my bracelet. "Yes, it is. Who the fuck is this?"

"My father," I hissed. "I tried to tell you."

His mouth snapped shut, and his features cleared of all emotion as he turned into Mr. King, the businessman. "General Carvene, you'll have to excuse me. I didn't recognize your voice."

My father snorted. "Yes, I could tell you were distracted by the way you were berating my daughter."

Godric's eyes peered skyward. He sighed heavily. "I imagine you have questions about what you overheard."

"I do. That can be saved for when I get there. We will talk in person then." My father hummed. "We can discuss something else now. That photo you are so upset about, the picture I wanted to burn my eyes out after seeing, was sent to me."

Godric's shoulders stiffened, and he stared at the intimate image. His tone flattened—a dangerous sound. "This was sent to you?"

"Yes. About a half hour ago. It's untraceable."

Godric's jaw clenched.

"Did you have guards outside the room?"

"Yes," he growled.

My father went silent, and then asked, "Are your men targeting my daughter or are we the targets?"

Smart, smart man.

He didn't jump to conclusions.

My father had one army. Godric had the other.

Spark a fire between the two, and there would be war again. Anyone wanting to take over would merely wait until they destroyed each other. No work done on their part other than sending a racy photo to an overprotective father.

Godric rubbed the back of his neck, his eyebrows furrowing in thought. "Was it just the photo sent?"

"Yes. There wasn't a note."

"Then it's probably us. I'll look into it."

"I'll expect a report," my father said, and then he switched topics. "I'll arrive in New City tomorrow. We'll talk then about private issues."

"Bye, Father," I quickly added.

"Call me if you need me before then. Goodbye."

He ended the call.

I quickly tapped my bracelet.

The image disappeared.

"Was it Jonathan?" I asked evenly.

Godric's nose scrunched. "Maybe."

"You're not sure?"

"No, I'm not. He's loyal to my father."

"Meaning?"

"No one fucks with my father. He would take great offense to someone trying to hurt me. So, essentially, being loyal to my father is being loyal to me too."

I nodded. "And it would be too obvious. Jonathan was the one interrupting us. If he's a clever person, he would have been certain not to put himself in a situation to be caught."

Godric stayed quiet for long moments before he blinked with a thought. "How exactly did you get out of my room without being seen by my guards?"

"There's a hidden passageway..." I trailed off, my eyes widening. I tapped my bracelet again and pulled up the image. I studied the angle further and pointed. "The bedroom door was more that way, wasn't it?"

Godric was bent, reviewing the photo too. His

golden eyes narrowed. "My men didn't take this."

"You're right." I nodded. "This was taken from the bathroom. That's where the hidden passageway is."

Godric straightened and crossed his arms over his chest. His lips curved in a pleased, evil grin. He chuckled ever so softly, and it was frightening. "That means it came from your father's, and there's only one man who would benefit directly from this."

My forehead crinkled. "His men are loyal."

"It's like a puzzle, pet. Think a second."

Deep in thought, I ate more nuts. I stared off into nothing as I thought about that night, replaying it in my mind. I thought about the people in power directly underneath my father. The people who knew about the passageways. I blinked as if I were waking up.

"It's Brandon." I jerked my excited regard to humored golden eyes. "My father said he arrived early. He saw you and me leave together after we were in the bar with your entourage of guards. All the soldiers know the layout of the base, and the higher-up officials are briefed with exit strategies in case of an attack. He would have known about the hidden passageways."

"Keep going..." Godric rested his hip against the counter, a proud glimmer in his eyes. "You've almost got this."

I shook my head in amusement. "He was getting intel on you. It's wasn't me. But he figured out who I was soon enough when we met. The girl with the great Mr. King was his own fiancée."

Godric rolled his finger. Waited.

"News has spread that I left my father to join the Corporate Army. The timing that my father received the image means that Brandon was keeping track to see if I was accepted or not. And he knows if we'd married, it would have sealed his future as the next general. But I was accepted into the CA, so no marriage for him." My brows bounced with the giddiness of being correct. "His future as a general was in jeopardy, so he took matters into his own hands. He wants my father dead so that he can secure his place again."

Godric slowly clapped. One. Two. Three.

Then he dipped and pressed his lips to mine.

His kiss was indulgent.

I grinned against his mouth. "So, big man, how did a man sneak into the bedroom with a shifter who has a great sense of smell?"

Godric nipped my bottom lip. "You tell me."

"The shifter was finally getting some after one hundred years of no pussy. He was a little preoccupied."

He chuckled, tilted his head to lick along my bottom lip. "You would be correct, pet."

A masculine throat cleared behind me.

I didn't want to move, so I didn't. I placed my forehead against Godric's chest and inhaled his unique scent while he straightened to deal with whoever had interrupted us. Wild spice and cherries surrounded me, calming my shattered nerves.

Godric's arms embraced my frame, his hands rubbing on my back in comfort. He stated gently, "Poppy?"

"I'm smelling you. Hold on."

He chuckled, his chest vibrating against my head.

I sighed. "You're ruining it."

"I'd like you to meet someone."

"Okay." I tipped my head back to stare into his eyes.

"It's my father."

CHAPTER THIRTY-FOUR

Inside Godric's warm embrace, I pivoted and placed my back against his chest, a warm smile on my face to greet his father.

The view had me stopping short in confusion.

And a little fear.

I sucked in a lungful of oxygen. "I don't understand."

A honey-haired man wearing a pair of orange swim trunks and a gray t-shirt stood before me. His muscles bulged under his beachwear attire, and black flip-flops graced his feet. His age was indistinguishable—maybe twenty, maybe thirty—but his penetrating dark eyes were still scary as hell.

"Poppy, this is my father, Theron King," Godric explained, a careful hum in his tone. The golden lion was being gentle with me. "Father, this is Poppy Carvene. She's my mate."

Immortal. They're all immortal.

I shivered again at the remembrance.

Theron's gaze honed on me with his son's words, his eyes narrowing. "Your mate?"

Scary, scary man.

"Yes, my mate. We figured it out today."

He strolled forward with strong legs.

I stiffened and pressed harder against Godric.

Theron's gaze never left mine. He dipped and leaned in toward me. His nostrils flared as he smelled my hair, my shoulders, and even ducked against my neck to sniff at my throat.

Weirdest parent meet-and-greet ever.

"Godric?" I asked, my voice shaking.

Theron was trailing his nose up my neck, smelling my skin the whole way. He huffed against my neck. Then his nose pressed harder, his chest expanding as he inhaled again.

Godric hugged me tighter. "It's okay, pet."

Theron pulled back and straightened.

His eyes were wide in surprise. "There's no darkness."

"I know," Godric said, his tone gentle.

Then I remembered Godric's mom.

One of the six matings that were magically wrong.

Theron blinked. "The curse is gone."

"It is." Godric laughed. "Now say hi to my mate."

Theron's gaze snapped down to me, and he smiled so wide I could see all of his teeth. And he was glorious, a beauty to behold. He lifted my right hand and bent to kiss the top of it gently before straightening again. "It is my truest pleasure to welcome you to the family, Poppy."

I yelped as he yanked me out of Godric's embrace and crushed me into a hug. My hands hung down by my sides, and the left side of my face crushed against his hard chest. I peeked out of the corner of my eye back to Godric.

He was grinning, his golden eyes full of joy. But his gaze was all for his father. He was elated by his father's sudden happiness, his shoulders relaxing.

I closed my eyes in resignation and lifted my hands. I hugged his father back, holding him around his lean waist. "I have to admit, Theron. You may frighten me, but you give a great hug."

* * *

Godric's mansion was impressive.

The three of us walked down many different

hallways on our way to where 'everyone' was meeting. They had decided on the living room. We had yet to get there, after walking for three minutes.

Godric typed on his bracelet, his gaze intent on it.

"What are you doing?" I leaned to peek.

"I'm informing your father about our theory."

My lips tilted up in a smile. "Thank you."

Theron walked behind us. "Poppy, your last name is Carvene. As in, General Carvene?"

Godric answered for me, sounding irritated. "Yes, her father is the man who attempts to thwart any new law I put into place."

I flicked a glare at him. "Then quit trying to put stupid laws into place. You're not the king of the world. The people should have a say in their well-being."

"The people shouldn't have tried to exterminate themselves. They obviously need guidance to stay alive."

Theron chuckled behind us. "Poppy, he is actually a king."

Godric's shoulders stiffened.

I snorted. "I kind of walked into that one."

"I'm not talking about his last name," Theron explained. "He is the alpha king of the shifters."

I jerked to a stop.

With inhuman reactions, they stopped with me.

Godric continued typing.

Theron waited patiently.

"Like, he rules your people?" I asked smoothly.

"Yes," Godric muttered. "The thing my father isn't telling you is, as there is only one seer living at a time, there should only be one alpha king. But instead, I was born. There are now two."

"What is an alpha king?" I glanced at him.

"The alpha with the most magical power."

I blinked. "Magical power to do what?"

"Control the shifters."

"Hmm." I nibbled on my bottom lip. "Who is the

other alpha king?"

"The man standing behind us."

My shoulders stiffened.

Theron laughed softly. "You have nothing to fear from me, Poppy. I handed over the crown to my son. I'm on vacation."

I blinked again. "A vacation means you'll be back."

Godric grunted.

"I ruled for over two thousand years. I'll be on vacation for a long time until I get bored. By then, my son will need a vacation."

"I already do," Godric muttered under his breath.

Theron patted his shoulder. "You're doing great, son."

I stared straight forward, unable to speak.

"Breathe, pet," Godric whispered.

I choked, "Two *thousand* years?"

Theron sighed. "I'm old. But I still look good."

A startled laugh burst from my throat. "I see where you get it from, big man. Like father like son." I looked behind me and evaluated his father again. "Does that mean you're a lion too?"

A private smile curved his lips. "No."

"What do you shift into?" I was curious.

He shrugged one shoulder, not answering.

Godric tapped the last bit into his bracelet. He grabbed my hand then and pulled me down the hallway.

His father followed, whistling quietly.

"Cassander's here," Godric stated, distracted.

His father replied, "I know. Are you all right?"

"I'm fine."

Even I knew that was a lie, his shoulders tensing.

"I wish you two would talk things through," his father crooned. "You were best friends, and then—"

"I know what happened, Father," Godric interjected. "I'm sorry, but I can't accept it like you did. Your mating may have been hell, but she was still

181

my mother."

Theron sighed. "He's hurting just as much as you are."

"Good," Godric growled.

CHAPTER THIRTY-FIVE

"Finally," Cassander grumbled.

Theron pushed past us at the entrance of the living room. He marched straight toward the seer, flicked his wrist, and ordered, "Get up, son. I haven't seen you in years."

The seer sighed in exasperation but pushed off the black couch. "Hi, Dad."

My eyebrows shot up in surprise.

Theron crushed him in a powerful hug.

I blinked and whispered, "Wait. He's your brother?"

"Adopted brother," Godric answered quietly. "My mother and father adopted him when his parents split up."

I jerked to face him. "I thought mates were forever."

"I can hear you two," Cassander muttered.

Theron released him from his embrace and patted his back hard. "You're coming to dinner in three days." He flicked a finger at the rest of the individuals in the room. "They've already been trapped into coming, thanks to your brother taking time off to follow his mate around for a few days." He swung his finger at the fox. "You *will* come."

Cassander ran his hands through his silver hair. "I think I have plans—"

"Bullshit. You're coming."

Cassander groaned. "Fine."

Theron slapped his shoulder. "I'll cook your favorite."

The seer perked up then. "Lasagna?"

Finn even looked up from his bracelet.

"Absolutely."

Godric grunted.

Cassander peeked at him under his lashes. "I'm still the favorite."

His lion took offense and growled.

I held tight to his hand when he stepped forward. "We have stuff to talk about. No fighting."

Dizzy. I was dizzy with all of this.

The man wearing orange swim trunks was ancient.

I was falling for a lion.

A stalker fox could kill them all.

Oh, and I was undying now.

It would take time to adjust to the crazy.

My eyes skimmed to the other three men. "Let me guess. You're shifters too."

Wolfe flicked his gray hair off his forehead. "Of course."

Rune leaned back in a recliner, rocking it back and forth slowly. His grin was sinful. "And you fucked God and reached immortality."

Alaric's chest rumbled with laughter. "Best nickname ever. Just for that line."

They high-fived one another.

Then Alaric turned his attention our way, his brown hair shining under the overhead light. "Congratulations, by the way. We heard she doesn't stink with the darkness. It's about damn time that shit ended."

Theron pegged each with a hard stare.

All three instantly went mute.

Theron proceeded to kick off his flip-flops, lie down on the floor, and put his hands under his head as a cushion. He stared at the ceiling and then closed his eyes as if he were taking a nap. Little grains of sand fell off his shoulders and onto the carpeting near his head. If someone walked in, he would appear like a tourist who was worn out from picking up seashells.

"This is just weird," I mumbled.

Godric pulled me close to his side, his golden eyes holding mine. "You'll get used to it."

Cassander fell back onto the couch. "Let's get this going. I'm getting hungry after all that lasagna talk."

I held up a finger. "Hold on. I know this is a delicate topic, but I need to ask. What did Godric mean when he said your parents split up?" I nibbled on my bottom lip in worry.

"They're still mated," he clarified. He was so patient when he talked with me. It was a kindness I appreciated. He explained further, "God told you about the six matings that were cursed. My parents are one of those matings."

"Mine too," Finn added.

"Same," Alaric supplied.

Rune grunted. "Crazy ass parents here too."

I glanced at Wolfe.

He nodded. "We're the offspring of the curse."

My brows rose. "All right."

Godric pulled me by my hand to the loveseat nearby. He sat down, and then pulled me onto his lap. His heat and scent wound around me in the most pleasant way. The lion man rubbed my back, massaging my muscles.

It was time to get down to business.

Godric growled. "Okay, here is what we know. Black creatures, no eyes, sharp claws, and stank like mud, tried to attack today. They weren't human or shifter."

"Golems," Cassander supplied. "I'm pretty sure they were golems."

"What's a golem?" Rune wrinkled his forehead.

"A creature formed by magic," I stated helpfully.

All six pairs of eyes snapped in my direction.

Theron didn't move from his 'nap' position.

"What? I like to read old books."

Cassander snickered. "She's right. It's a magical creature created by clay and then animated to life."

Finn asked, "So someone is behind it?"

Cassander continued to give his knowledge. "They would have to be, but I'm not sure who."

My brows furrowed.

On the field, Cassander had said, 'The bastard must be weak.'

"But it's a male, right?" I asked carefully.

He answered, "Yes, it would have to be a shifter. Humans aren't magical."

My eyes narrowed. "Before the fight, you said he was weak. How do you not know who it is but then claim to know he's weak?"

"Because I could make golems like that, and they would be a hell of a lot faster."

"You can do that?" I asked in confusion.

He smirked. "I'm the seer. There are a few perks."

"But no other shifter can?"

"Exactly."

"Then it's a puzzle." Giddiness rose inside my chest. But, just as suddenly, it disappeared with my next thought. "I dreamt about them this morning. They were trying to get me. And they had this weird green glow coming out of their mouths that was almost hypnotic—it felt wrong."

Godric tightened his arms around me, his attention snapping to his brother. "Is that normal, Cass?"

"If it's magical, and she was the target, she may

have experienced the backlash of the magic when the creatures were made. Especially since the creator is weak."

"So I have a shifter on my hands who is fucking with magic," Godric stated. His voice remained even and cool...and underneath simmered with a burial sentence. "It's possible the curse and this are related. Before, we thought our race might be ending. But twice? And different? Someone is twisting magic to target mates."

Finn held a blade in his hand, tossing it back and forth from one hand to the other. "We need to compile a list of shifters who have been known to hate mates—the idea of mates. And shifters who are obsessive about them. That would be the first place to start."

Wolfe agreed. "I'll start a search in the database."

"One good thing about all of this is he's weak," Cassander stated. "The more he twists the magic, the less effective it'll be. It will drain him and not work as it should. And with as many golems as he sent today, he thinks a lot of himself. That will eventually be his downfall if he doesn't change his course of attack."

"Do you think Poppy is in danger right now?" Godric asked, his voice soft. He was glaring at his brother as if it pained him to ask for advice. But his attention didn't waver from him. "Should you stay here to help me protect her?"

I glowed inside.

He cared. He cared enough to humble himself.

Cassander cleared his throat and picked at the fur on his jacket. "No, she's not in danger right now. With that much magic spent, he'll be comatose for at least a month." He glanced up, his own voice quieting. "But...I could actually use a place to stay for a little while. I won't be in your way."

I held very still.

Cassander was obviously testing the waters.

Seeing if peace was in the near future for them.

Godric stared, his features calm.

Cassander cleared his throat, poking the lion.

It was never wise to poke a lion.

"I have a new mate." Godric shrugged. "I'd like to have the house to ourselves."

"Jesus," Finn muttered in annoyance. He glared at the lion and then turned his attention to the fox. "Cass, you can stay at my place for a while if you need to."

"Thank you." Cassander yawned. "I should have asked you first. I'd never get any sleep here with the way God snores. When the walls are shaking—and not from having sex—the man has issues."

Alaric chuckled and nodded his head. "Amen."

Godric glared. "You are such an asshole, Cass."

"Please," he muttered with sarcasm. "You're just embarrassed because it's the truth, and you're afraid your mate won't sleep with you every night once she hears it."

Wolfe glanced at me. "Bring earplugs to bed."

"I actually snore too. He'll need his own set of earplugs. My father listens to music at night when I'm there so he can get some rest."

Godric's eyes captured mine. "You really snore?"

"Oh, yeah. It's bad."

The wrinkles of worry vanished from his forehead, and he smiled, the corners of his eyes crinkling. "The magic picked well. Because the asshole is right. I snore like the devil when I'm stressed."

My lips curved. He was quite adorable.

Rune groaned. "They're cute and shit."

Alaric muttered, "I hope he finds his balls when he returns to work. I can't put up with him smiling all the time like that."

Godric leaned down and kissed my lips softly. "I think it's time for them to leave. What do you think, pet?"

"It's your house. Your rules."

Cassander's head cocked. "I just thought of something."

"It's a miracle," Godric rumbled.

"Fuck off," Cassander groused absently. His silver eyes swung in my direction. "You said the golems had green light in their mouths?"

I nodded.

"That would have to do with the soul."

"Huh?" He was talking gibberish.

"Twisting the magic to darkness," he mumbled to himself, staring at his lap. He tapped his thumbs together, lost in thought. "What did the green light do, Ms. Carvene?"

"Poppy," I corrected him.

"Apologies." Silver eyes looked up and refocused. "Did the green light do anything other than appear to be hypnotic, like you said?"

I nibbled on my bottom lip. "It was kind of all-consuming. That's the best way I can explain it."

His eyes narrowed. "I know what it is."

Wolfe asked, "What?"

"The golems were meant to suck the soul from her."

I jerked back in surprise. "That would have killed me, wouldn't it have?"

A soul was a soul. It couldn't be reformed.

What you had was what you got. Immortal or not.

"Kind of," he hedged. "Your body would still be living, but no one would be in residence. Once the soul leaves the body, it doesn't return."

Godric hissed, "How sure are you on this?"

"Almost positive. It makes the most sense with everything I've learned from watching souls leave bodies."

I stared, my mouth gaping. "You see their souls?"

He nodded. For a brief second, his silver eyes were haunted. Then he chuckled, with a smile. "The bastards are always green too. Like, neon fucking green."

Theron decided to speak, his eyes still closed. "Is that all for tonight, gentlemen?"

Godric muttered, "I hope to hell it is."

No one else spoke with concerns, the room quiet.

"Time to go then." Theron jumped to his feet, sliding his flip-flops on, entirely cheerful. Then he snapped his fingers at the other men, his dark eyes narrowing to dangerous slits and his tone lowering to a snarl. "Get the hell out of here before you piss me off. Give the newly mated pair some privacy."

It was like whiplash how fast he altered himself.

They jumped to their feet, hauling ass outside.

He barked after them, "I will see you all for dinner in three days. Don't forget. I'm making lasagna!"

Hilarity bubbled inside my chest.

Without moving his lips, Godric whispered on a mere breath, "Don't laugh. That actually will piss him off."

I shoved any laughter down deep.

I did not want to make that man mad.

Theron sighed and turned patient eyes on his son. "You should have let him stay here. He was waving a damn white flag in the air."

Godric's nose scrunched. "I know."

"Then get your shit together. You're better than this," his father scolded. He shook his head of honey-colored hair. "Anyway, I'm leaving too. I'm off for my dance class. There's this amazing elderly couple who I just adore there."

With unblinking eyes, I watched him leave.

"Godric?"

He chuckled. "I know what you're going to ask."

"Is he always like that?" I asked it anyway.

"Yes, he is."

"Wow." I nodded like I understood. But I didn't think anyone would understand a man who had lived for two thousand years. "Do we really need to go to dinner—"

"You are going!" Theron shouted from far outside the room.

I snapped my mouth shut.

Godric winked. "Shifter hearing, pet."

CHAPTER THIRTY-SIX

"So…" My voice was suddenly quiet. "What now?"

Godric's lips curled with a secret only he knew. He lifted his right hand and pointed a finger over the top of my left hand, just a sliver away from touching. The heat burned my skin, and I shivered as he ran his finger up and down my arm slowly, not allowing me to feel his flesh on mine but gifting me the warmth.

He purred, "My bedroom is right through that door in the corner. I had the meeting here to be closer to it."

My voice was breathless as I watched his finger trail up and down my arm. "That was proactive." I licked my bottom lip. "But do I need to go back to the Military House tonight?"

"No, I've already contacted them. We'll go there tomorrow before I have to go to work. We'll pick up your personal items. You also have forms you need to fill out to officially join the CA."

I wanted to grab that finger. "I need to sign-up for the intelligence unit's exam, too."

"I read in your file that's where you wanted to be placed. I think you'll be a good fit there if you pass the exam."

"You read my file?"

"Of course."

He leaned over and bit my shoulder. Just a love bite. With his teeth holding on, he grinned up at me. His finger finally touched my flesh, dipping under the sleeve of my t-shirt. He ran the pad of his finger in lazy circles on my skin.

I closed my eyes. "You are going to ruin me."

He let go of my shoulder and placed his lips against my throat, whispering, "In the best possible way."

Godric lifted me into his arms as he stood, carrying me to his bedroom. He placed me gently on his bed and stared down at me with sensual hunger in his golden eyes.

I sucked in a harsh breath as he silently undressed me. His fingers brushed my sides, the tops of my breasts, my inner thighs, and the side of my neck. I trembled underneath his light touches.

The comforter was soft beneath my body as he lifted and resituated me, placing me in the center of the mattress.

He removed his clothing just as slowly as he had mine, standing on the side of the bed. His golden eyes devoured all of my skin on display, his chest heaving by the time he crawled over me.

I expected the soft touch. I shouldn't have.

He grabbed a fistful of my hair and yanked my head back, his mouth landing on my neck.

I groaned in pleasure, "Godric."

He nipped my neck softly, even while he kept his brutal hold on my hair. "You smell so damn good. Like home and sex and passion."

"Cherries are better," I moaned.

I ran my fingers down his flexing back muscles.

Godric chuckled and pressed his hard chest against mine. The heat from his skin was scorching, and the scent of him overrode thought. He ran his free hand down my side to pull my leg over his hip and ground his erection against my wet core, pressing against my clit with each thrust of his hips. His cock was soon coated in my wetness, and I trembled under him, wanting him now.

He moaned in pleasure, his fist tightening in my

hair. His face lifted and hovered over mine, his breath fanning my face. Only pure carnal need etched his hard features as he touched his lips to mine, his tongue surging into my mouth, exploring his mate with abandon.

It was intoxicating.

I lifted my face up as much was allowed with his cruel grip in my hair, and shoved harder against his lips, craving the man who I was bound to forever.

The lion inside him growled, and he tipped his hips back, placing his cock at the entrance of my soaking core. Even while he ate at my mouth like he was starving, he pushed his cock inside me ever so slowly.

I rocked my hips, trying to get him inside me faster, needing to be filled and fucked with his large cock.

"So greedy," he whispered, biting my jaw.

His hips pumped a little faster, almost all the way inside me. He was torturing and teasing me.

"Fuck me," I begged.

He drew his hips back, retreating. Staying there.

"No," I cried out, arching against his body.

He chuckled and thrust home with savage strength.

"Oh, yes!"

His teeth bit down on the side of my neck, and he pulled his hips back, only to slam back into me once more. Repeatedly, he pounded into my pussy, stretching me full of the most perfect cock in existence. He growled against my neck, his teeth biting harder, and his muscles bulging in exertion.

I gripped his shoulders and dug my fingernails into his skin, the wetness and heat of tiny drops of blood on my fingertips.

Godric shoved into my channel faster, his breath coming in hard pants against my neck. He released his bite and licked along my neck. His voice was breathless as he whispered, "My mate."

I nodded my head, delirious with pleasure.

He slanted his hips, grinding against my clit with each plunge. His face lifted over mine, watching as the fever inside my veins started to boil. Sweat glistened on our skin. The slapping of our bodies joining was loud inside his bedroom.

"Godric," I whispered, my mind tipping

"I've got you." His lips kissed my cheek softly.

Jarring ecstasy slammed from within my body.

I shook with each pounding of the crashing waves.

My eyes locked with his as I sank into the warmth.

He shuddered over me, sinking his cock deep.

His teeth clenched with his climax. The muscles in his arms trembled, and his cock pumped his release inside my channel. His nostrils flared as he inhaled our scent together.

I jerked in aftershocks of tingling pleasure, and his large frame crashed down onto mine, his head hitting the pillow in the afterglow.

I angled my head against his, resting it there, and attempted to regain my breathing. I flexed my fingers, releasing the cutting hold I had on his shoulders. The tips of my fingers were red and damp with his blood.

I grinned and closed my eyes. "You're good."

His chest was still pumping heavily with much-needed oxygen, but it shook in humor as he laughed lightly, his words muffled against the pillow. "Thank you. So are you, pet."

CHAPTER THIRTY-SEVEN

Godric and I stepped off his private train in front of the Military House, just as Finn was hopping down from his own train.

Finn slapped Godric on the shoulder. "Have a good night?"

Godric flinched and glared.

Finn's brows pulled together. He moved with inhuman speed and pulled the neck of Godric's simple t-shirt to the side. The white-haired tiger stared at the little puncture wounds on Godric's left shoulder.

"Cut it out," Godric growled.

Finn snickered and fixed his friend's shirt. "It looks like you did have a good night."

We'd had an excellent night.

Shifters could go *all night long*.

"That is private," Godric hissed and pulled my body against his side with his arm protectively around my waist. "What we do in the bedroom is none of your damn business."

Finn smirked. "You're already possessive as hell."

"She's mine. End of story."

My face heated with a pink blush. "Let's just go inside. It's chilly out this morning."

Finn opened the gate to the Military House with a touch of his bracelet against the lock. "What are you guys doing here this morning, anyway?"

"Picking up my stuff. Why are you here?"

He chuckled. "Same reason."

"I'm leaving mine here." Godric shrugged. "They can donate it. I didn't have anything of importance with me. Just clothes."

"That's very generous of you, kind leader."

"Fuck off, Finn. It's too damn early."

He blinked. "You were up all night, weren't you?"

Godric's golden eyes speared his. "What did I just say about my sex life being private?"

Finn smirked. "It is so fun to tease you when you're sleep deprived."

"Well, stop it," Godric groused.

"Okay...I bet you didn't get the chance to snore."

Godric's fist shot out, punching his friend's shoulder hard enough to knock him back a step. "Keep teasing. We'll see who's laughing at the end of the day."

We ambled up the walkway, the birds chirping nearby once again near the Military house. There had to be a nest somewhere. At least they didn't poop all over the walkway.

Major Wilcox was waiting for us inside the foyer.

Her eyes wandered over Godric and me.

But she didn't comment on the way he held me close.

The white splint on her nose was garish. With her broken nose, it sounded like she had a bad cold while she spoke. "Ms. Carvene, I need to give you the forms for your official invitation to the Corporate Army."

I grinned, my cheeks pinching. "I'm very excited."

Her lips twitched. "You're the only recruit to ever break an instructor's nose. You deserve to be in the CA. You'll do just fine with us."

"Thank you." I bounced inside Godric's embrace. "When can I take the exam for the intelligence unit?"

"There's actually one tomorrow. The one after that isn't for another two months."

My eyes widened. "I don't think I'll be prepared for an exam tomorrow. I'll need to study."

"Smart, Ms. Carvene. You don't want your

enthusiasm hindering your test score."

"I'll sign up for the one in two months then."

Godric glanced down into my eyes. "Do you want me to go pack your bag while you take care of your business? I need to be at work in an hour."

I nodded. "Thank you. That's helpful."

He bent to kiss my lips gently, and then he slammed his hand down on Finn's shoulder. "You have to be at work in an hour too. Let's get this shit done."

They began walking up the stairs.

I snapped my fingers, saying, "Don't forget my hat."

He waved a hand behind him, exhaustion apparent in the set of his shoulders. "I know. I know."

The major watched the exchange in silence.

When they were all the way upstairs, she whispered in confusion, "How the hell did that happen?"

I shrugged a shoulder. "Magic."

* * *

I poked my head up off Godric's couch. There was a tapping at the front door. I rubbed my eyes and stood. I tapped my bracelet, making the image of the intelligence unit's study material disappear.

I tapped it again. "Order: Call Godric Leon."

I needed to change his name sometime on there. Maybe, Sexy Beast.

"I'm in a meeting," he said by way of answering.

The man needed sleep.

I wouldn't deprive him of a full night again.

"There's someone at your door. Are you expecting company?"

"No," he answered. "Don't answer it."

Tap. Tap. Tap.

"They aren't leaving."

"I'll look at the cameras. Just a second."

Tap. Tap. Tap. Tap. Tap.

Godric grunted. "Fuck. It's your father."

My eyes widened. "I thought he would call first and meet us somewhere!"

"You're not thinking about the important part." He growled. "He's got a tracking device set in your bracelet. That's the only way he would know where to find you right now."

Bang. Bang. Bang.

"He's getting upset. I need to answer it."

"I'm already on my way. I'll be there shortly."

The call ended.

I pushed my shoulders back. "I can do this."

By the time I answered the door, I swear he was kicking it. I opened it wide, a smile on my face. I said in a sweet voice, "Hello, Father."

His features instantly calmed, relief showing.

"I wasn't kidnapped. Settle down."

"When you have a girl, I hope she gives you hell."

I snorted. "Are you going to come in?"

"First, whose house is this?" he asked, and then he pointed to the statue next to him. "And who the fuck puts something this ridiculous outside their home?"

I laughed for so long, I had tears rolling down my cheeks. I moved and grabbed him in a hug. He may not win any awards for tender parenting, but he was my blood.

I whispered, "I missed you, Father."

His arms wrapped around my back, squeezing me tight. "I missed you too, darling dearest."

When I finally let go, he released me.

He stepped backward and tipped his head up, surveying the structure. "So, answer my question. Whose home is this?"

A train landed on the plot past the walkway.

I pointed a finger at it. "It's his."

My father swiftly turned around.

Godric's form appeared in the doorway.

He stared right at us.
My father groaned. "God, I hate him."

CHAPTER THIRTY-EIGHT

"This is awkward. One of you two need to speak," I muttered in frustration. The kitchen was sunny and bright, perfectly acceptable for positive moods. "It's been ten minutes, and all we've done is stare at one another."

Godric grunted.

My father stared hard at him.

"I'm going to take a nap if no one is talking."

Godric scowled directly into my eyes. "If I don't sleep, you don't sleep."

"You know what, big man? You have been a sourpuss all day. If I had known you were this big of a baby without a little shut-eye, I would have slept on the damn couch."

My father raised one brow. "So other than the fact the two of you are having sex, you're now staying here, Poppy?"

I nibbled on my bottom lip. "Um... I can't answer that."

Godric glared again. "Why not? You know you're staying here. This is your home now."

I threw my hands up into the air. "Because you haven't asked me yet! I told you yesterday you needed to ask."

"Really?" he droned.

"Yes, really."

He ground his teeth together, his golden eyes

scanning my face. "Fine. Do you want to move in with me?"

"Yes. Thank you for asking." I smiled sweetly.

Godric peered down his nose. "You didn't eat yet, did you?"

"I was studying. I lost track of time."

"You look like shit. Get something.

"You're such a sweet talker."

His brows furrowed. "Really, get something to eat."

I blinked. He was worried about me.

And I was immortal.

He might be more overprotective than my father was.

"Do you want something?" I asked.

He rubbed his forehead and sighed. "Actually, a cup of coffee would be great."

I nodded and walked to the counter, glancing at my father. "Do you want a cup?"

My father blinked. Twice. "I'll take something a little harder if it's available."

Godric rested more comfortably on his chair and tossed his arm over the back of mine. "I've got a bottle of whiskey."

My father looked back to where I was working on the coffee machine. "I want the whole bottle."

I chuckled. "I'll get you two shots of whiskey and a cup of coffee."

"I guess that'll have to do." My father turned his attention to the person he really wanted to speak with. "Tell me, Mr. King, how in the hell do you think this is actually going to work? While it appears you two have fallen head over heels for each other, you and I are still on opposite sides of every world view. Ideals, I might add, my daughter also agrees with."

Godric cracked his neck, the popping noise like wood breaking. "I'm doing what I believe is best for the entire populace of the world—"

My father jerked his hand up in a stopping

gesture. "I don't want to talk business, Mr. King. I want to know how you actually believe this personal relationship is going to work."

Godric stared into his eyes. "Like any other relationship does. With bumps and bruises. I can't tell you a perfect fix for this situation." He shook his head of tawny curls. "I've fallen for a woman who is funny and intelligent and strong and beautiful. I didn't want to. My parents' marriage was so fucked up that I never wanted a relationship. But as soon as I met Poppy, I started falling. I won't let her go now. I care too deeply for her to do that."

I slowly shut my gaping mouth.

My hand looked a little ridiculous halfway up in the air with a spoonful of cold macaroni, so I quickly stuffed the food into my mouth. I chewed and aimed a direct glare at my father.

He was upsetting Godric. I didn't like that.

My father rubbed his chin, glanced at me, and then looked back to the man across from him. "You two are very different. Do you believe it will work long-term?"

"Are you asking if I'm going to marry her?"

I froze in place, another bite of macaroni caught in mid-air.

My father shrugged. "Is that a possibility?"

"When I think she's ready, I'll ask her."

I ate my bite, chewing slowly.

My father looked into my eyes.

I nodded. I approved of his answer.

My father raised his eyebrows in surprise, but he glanced to Godric. His features shut down, his expression stone cold. "I have one personal question of my own. One I've never asked you, and perhaps I should have. Did you know there was a glitch in your system? Were you just cutting corners to make more money?"

I held my breath.

Godric didn't flinch. He stated, "I didn't know

about the glitch that failed your wife. I would never have held back lifesaving supplies. There are plenty of cities now that continue to receive medical equipment, even when they are millions of units behind in payments."

I exhaled heavily, a lifetime of accusation lifted from my shoulders. I poured the brewed coffee and the whiskey. The two men were quite still as I set the multiple cups on the table.

On my way back to the counter, I squeezed Godric's shoulder in appreciation. My father and I had both needed to hear that. He grabbed my hand and squeezed it back, letting my palm slide out of his grasp as I walked to get my food.

Godric murmured respectfully, "I've never said this before either. And I should have. I am truly sorry for the loss of your wife, General Carvene."

My father sucked in a large breath.

I put my macaroni down on the table and instantly rushed to my father's side. I leaned over and threw my arms around him. My father trembled in my arms, tucking his head against my shoulder, and held me with strong arms.

A tear had slipped down his cheek.

I had only seen him cry once—by my mom's hospital bed when there was nothing left to do to save her.

My eyes burned as I rubbed his back.

"I think I have an idea, Father," I whispered. "A way to make everyone believe you accept our relationship on a personal level but not on a professional level."

His head lifted, and his eyes were thankfully dry now. "What has my darling dearest come up with now?"

"You'll see."

* * *

"I cannot believe you talked me into this," Godric whispered the next day through a fake smile plastered on his face. He lifted his hand and flicked his wrist in a small wave to the photographers outside the restaurant's window. His eyes returned to mine. "How many times do we have to do this?"

"At least once every two months," I answered primly. I pointed to the food on his plate. "Eat something, or they'll think you're not having fun."

My father chuckled as he leaned back in his chair. He was enjoying Godric's discomfort immensely. We were in Port, definitely not New City. This was saving my father's reputation with his army. He chewed a baby potato and swallowed it before stating, "The food is excellent here. Relax and enjoy it."

Godric grumbled under his breath but started cutting into his steak. "You should probably lean over and kiss me. They need to know we're a couple, and I'm not just here schmoozing with your father and his daughter."

My lips twitched.

He wanted to save face with his own subordinates too.

I leaned on my chair in his direction, and he looked up, completely attuned to my body. His head dipped, and he pressed his lips to mine for a chaste but loving kiss. I leaned back on my chair and cleared my throat.

My father muttered, "I may have lost my appetite."

"Don't look disgusted or you'll ruin this," I mumbled, with a smile on my face. I took a drink of wine from my glass, asking behind it, "Did they take a picture of that?"

My father snorted and scanned his plate for his next bite. "Yes. My guess is it will be everywhere within the next five minutes."

"My plan will work. I promise. Have a little faith."

"Speaking of work," my father probed. "When do

you start the CA officially?"

"In a week. I'm actually excited. Major Wilcox wants me on the investigation team until I take the intelligence unit's exam. There have apparently been a few women who have gone missing, and they want additional help. The major wanted me sooner, but the forms for enrollment in the CA take a while to get approval through their system."

My father's brows furrowed. "Can't Mr. King ask them to put a rush on it?"

Godric muttered, "Poppy is being very difficult—"

I poked his side. Hard. "You will not interfere with my job. No matter what."

Godric shrugged, his attention on my father. "See? Difficult."

"Promise me, Godric," I demanded.

I pouted. He had better not interfere.

My chin even trembled and my chest constricted. I wanted to do this on my own. I needed it.

Godric instantly set his utensils down and cupped my cheeks. His thumb ran over my lower lip, his forehead crinkled in dismay. "I won't. I promise, pet."

I heaved a sigh of relief, my eyes lighting with joy. "Thank you."

"You're welcome." Godric leaned down and kissed my lips softly, and then he lowered his hands from my face and picked up his utensils again.

My father instantly started laughing.

Both of our heads snapped in his direction.

He shook his head and pointed his fork. "You, Mr. King, are screwed. My daughter already has you wrapped around her little finger."

Godric's lips trembled. "Her little fingers are cute."

I cleared my throat pointedly to shut them down. "Father, what happened with Brandon? Was he behind the photo, as I suspected?"

"He was." Father ate another potato.

"What did you do with him?"

My father grinned, calm and happy. "I buried him."

CHAPTER THIRTY-NINE

"Shift for me." I bounced on the balls of my feet near the shoreline. We were back in New City at our home. My plan had worked as I'd hoped—all was good with my father and Godric now. And I was ready to see a lion. I wiggled my ball cap, adjusting the bill. "Come on. Show me."

Godric's brows rose. "Right here?"

"You're a lion. Is anyone around?"

He cocked his head, listened, and inhaled deeply. His head tipped back into the late afternoon sun, closing his eyes, beautiful in all ways. The man was in his element, wild and fierce as he used his inhuman senses.

"So?" I asked with excitement.

Godric opened his golden eyes and stared into the very heart of me. His lips curved as he scanned my eager features. "No one's around."

I punched a fist into the air. "Let me see, big man."

"Fine. But don't be frightened. It's still me."

He kicked off his tennis shoes and removed his t-shirt at the same time. My little claw marks on his shoulders were still there, scabbed over, healing normally. His shorts were taken off last, and he wore no underwear.

He was gloriously naked in front of me, the water lapping gently near our feet.

An explosion of white sparkles erupted.

I skittered backward.

That was much more than Cassander's had been.

I blinked. A lion sat before me.

"Oh my," I whispered in awe. "You're big."

The lion pushed up to all four paws.

And proceeded to strut in a circle, his tail flicking.

I snickered. "You are so damn vain."

His tail twitched.

I wasn't frightened at all. I trusted my man.

I moved forward, placed my hands on his tawny fur, and stroked down his massive mane. "It's coarse but still soft. Like your normal hair."

Large golden eyes closed as I scratched my fingers down into his fur, rubbing all over him. He huffed an odd purr, starting and stopping in spurts. It was completely adorable.

The lion ducked and moved far back.

Then he started a low creep, almost on his belly, the muscles working under his fur. He hunted me, his eyes watching my every move, while he came closer.

I started backing up, grinning from ear to ear.

I turned...and tripped.

But I shoved myself up quickly enough and raced down the shoreline. I laughed and glanced over my shoulder, watching as the lion galloped at a slow pace behind me.

Then he raced past me and turned.

He started his slow creep again, low to the ground.

I pivoted and raced back the way I'd come.

The lion galloped around me in circles.

Again and again.

I held up my hand, breathless. "You're making me dizzy." I pointed to the sand. "Let's take a break."

The lion instantly rolled to his side.

The sand was cool beneath my touch as I sat down in front of him, and then I leaned back to rest my head on his shoulder. The water rippled, and the sky was a brilliant shade of purple on the horizon.

Content with my life, I whispered, "The sunset is beautiful."

His tail flicked twice, whacking onto the sand. We watched the sunset, as we were, peaceful in ourselves together. The warmth of his body was enough to keep me toasty warm against the chill.

* * *

Dinner was surprisingly nice with his father. I couldn't understand now why everyone acted like it was such a hindrance. His father had been quiet, but everyone else had talked and enjoyed themselves.

And damn, his father could cook.

Godric took off his dinner jacket and dropped it on the back of his father's couch, getting comfortable for drinks afterward. He untucked his shirt and unbuttoned the top button, and as an afterthought, he removed his weapon from the back of his pants and stuffed it in his jacket.

He kissed my cheek. "What would you like to drink?"

"Just a beer." My stomach was so full I didn't want anything hard on it.

The muscles under his shirt flexed as he walked with Finn to the long sidebar on the far side of the room. The rest of the gang already had their drinks and were now sitting down.

Curiosity overtook me.

I picked up the weird 'weapon' he always carried by the barrel, swinging it up and catching it. I repeated the action. I asked loudly, "Godric, why do you carry this useless thing around with you? A blade makes more sense."

I tossed it up and caught it again.

The occupants of the room froze.

Godric's hands shot up in the air. "Stop!"

Finn slid in front of Godric, blocking my view of him.

My brows furrowed at the protective action. I lifted the 'weapon' by the barrel and waved it in front of me. I sputtered, "Whatever this is, it's broken. There's no blade in the little barrel." I flipped it around and held it by the handle, pointing the barrel around the room so each person could see there was nothing inside it.

Rune choked on his drink. "Oh, my fuck. Someone take that away from her before she shoots one of us." He paused. "Or kills God if the bullet goes through Finn."

"What?" I asked, my forehead crinkling.

Theron walked toward me with his hands up in peace, his tone gentle and his eyes patient. "Let me have that, Poppy. Then we'll explain."

I jerked my hand in his direction. "Here."

Theron tensed, but he walked forward and carefully took the 'weapon' from my hand. He jerked his head in the direction of the bar. His voice was sharp and ticked. "Godric, get your ass over here and explain what this is."

Godric stepped from behind Finn.

He shook his head at me and strolled forward.

Theron handed him the 'weapon' and then smacked him upside his head. "She could have killed you."

His father marched away to his seat, glaring the whole way. He sat down with a huff and took a heavy swig of his liquor. He muttered, "Fucking kids."

I stared wide-eyed. "Godric, what the hell is that?"

My man sighed heavily and turned away from me. He lifted the weapon, clicked a little piece on it, and stuck his finger in the small loop. "Cover your ears, pet."

I did. The rest of the room did too, with scowls.

He squeezed his finger.

I jumped and screamed in fucking terror as the worst sound jarred my hearing and a bottle of clear

211

liquid on the sidebar exploded. I shouted in horror, "What the hell is that?"

Godric clicked the little piece on the side and placed the *definite* weapon into the back of his pants again. His gaze was patient on mine. "I'm sure you read about these in your history books. It's called a gun."

I slapped my hand over my mouth. "Holy shit."

He nodded and cupped my right cheek with his hand. "They are very dangerous and can kill easily. So until I've trained you to use it, don't touch it again. Do you understand?"

I nodded and dropped my hand from my mouth. "Those have been banned and illegal since the end of the war. They were confiscated from every remaining household and destroyed. How do you have one?"

His lips twitched. "Who do you think passed the law to ban them?"

My jaw dropped. "You?"

"Yes."

"And you kept some?"

"Of course."

I blinked. "I want one."

He chuckled. "Maybe once you learn how to handle it."

My eyes sparkled with delight.

He held up a finger. "I said maybe. Not yes." His brows rose. "After all, you nearly killed me a second ago."

I peered down my nose at him. "Not my fault. I didn't know what it was."

Godric stepped closer, running his palm over my waist to my back and pulling my body closer. His voice was an intimate, quiet purr of foreplay. "I'll show you a few new things tonight. Don't worry, pet. You'll be well-informed."

"Promise?" A small smile lifted my lips.

"Oh, yes. I promise."

My body hummed with warmth, all for him.

He inhaled deeply, his golden eyes flaring. He grinned, and whispered, "You like me."

"Shut it." I slapped his arm.

He winked. "I like you, too."

We were in love. We both knew it.

I'd fallen for a lion man.

He'd fallen for his enemy's daughter.

We couldn't be happier...

Unless we were in bed all day.

Cassander muttered, "Fucking hell, get a room, you two. You're stinking up the place with your lovey-dovey shit."

Godric muttered, "Screw you, Cass."

"Kids, no fighting," Theron ordered. He sipped at his drink, watching over the group. "Everyone needs to save their fight for when it's actually necessary. One day, we will take down the monster who is fucking with mates."

THE END

TRANSCEND

The bestselling, groundbreaking Origin series continues with Transcend. Women are disappearing in New City, and the Corporate Army assigns their best soldiers to the case. In a world still recovering from war and death, every woman is needed for the survival of the human race.

Mina Kramer is a socialite in New City. She smiles for her father's business associates, laughs at all their jokes, and acts the perfect daughter. When she's suddenly abducted from a party at Baker Corporation, her whole world turns sideways. The kidnappers aren't asking for her family's money, the one item her parents have plenty of. With only confusion and captivity in her future, she prays for a rescue by her parents.

Except her saviors come in the form of the all-power Mr. Finn Baker and Poppy Carvene, a tiny sprite of a woman. And they don't return her to her parents. Mr. Baker decides he wants to keep her and use her as bait to flush out the kidnappers' leader.

Mina must push her fears aside or dive deeper into them. Does she want to run to her parents, who are safe? Or will she transcend to a woman who fights criminals bent on destroying New City? And can she overcome her startling feelings for the sexy Mr. Baker, a man who harbors secrets of his own?

New York Times bestselling author and award-winner, Scarlett Dawn, is the author of the Forever Evermore new adult fantasy series, the Origin paranormal dystopian stories, the Mark new adult science fiction saga, and the Lion Security contemporary series.

Website http://www.scarlettdawn.net
Newsletter http://eepurl.com/4X1rv

48095537R00123

Made in the USA
San Bernardino, CA
16 April 2017